MICHAL'

DAUGHTER OF SAUL, WIFE OF DAVID

Hauton B. (Brandy) Lee

PublishAmerica
Baltimore

© 2002 by Hauton B. Lee, Jr.

All rights reserved. No part of this book may be reproduced in any form without written permission from the publishers, except by a reviewer who may quote brief passages in a review to be printed in a newspaper or magazine.

First printing

ISBN: 1-59129-790-7
PUBLISHED BY PUBLISHAMERICA BOOK PUBLISHERS
www.publishamerica.com
Baltimore

Printed in the United States of America

Thank you so much !

Prime Motivators & Academic Resources
Drs. Susie & John Stanley

Video Interview Of Author
(Before pagination revision)
Marilyn Dennis, Interviewer,
Renee Lewis, Response
Dr. Bill Pynne, Direction, Camera, and everything.

Reading, Suggestions,& Encouragement
Susan Hook, Lynette Hutchinson, Marydith Hooker, Rev. Larry Ortman, Helen Ryan, Gary & Becky Walker, Mary Wilcox

Special Presence & Assistance
Orla Hobson Lee, lifetime motivator, Leland (technical advice & assistance) & Esther Lee, Janet & Bob Hargis, Kristen Lee, Lisa & Michael Lawson, Nancy Lee, Christopher, Brian, & Jennifer Hargis, Evellyn Reed, Mary Shrock Rev. Sam & Adele Hooker, Clem Ryan, Dr. Jay & Jan Barber

A novel for every woman …
and every man who loves a woman.

FOREWORD		7
CHAPTER I	PAPA SAUL AND I	9
CHAPTER II	THE FABRIC OF A WORN CLOAK	42
CHAPTER III	BEHOLD I HAVE SEEN A SON OF JESSE	74
CHAPTER IV	THE FIRST WIFE OF DAVID	89
CHAPTER V	FOLLOWING DAVID'S TRAIL	102
CHAPTER VI	MICHAL'S FATE DECIDED	106
CHAPTER VII	MORE OF DAVID'S SCRAMBLING	109
CHAPTER VIII	DAVID AGAIN MEETS A GIANT	125
CHAPTER IX	DAVID'S WOMEN	128
CHAPTER X	DAVID'S POWER AND MORALITY	136
CHAPTER XI	CHASING DAVID AGAIN, ALONE	143
CHAPTER XII	DAVID, KING OF JUDAH, ONE TRIBE FOLLOWED HIM	154
CHAPTER XIII	KING OF ALL ISRAEL, AIDED BY RISPAH	165
CHAPTER XVI	DAVID SLEEPS WITH HIS FATHERS	181
CHAPTER XV	LOVE AND REVENGE SHARE THE SAME TENT	184

FOREWORD

I (Michal') lived with innocent youths as they became great men, while mixing sin and faith extravagantly. *If you hear me out, you'll not again see women the same, papa and David, too, for they were fallible as well as hungry for God.*

Kings Saul and David, in turn, did good and bad, twisted their lives and those of our people, in the process Israel tore up the landscape and themselves, began something that will change all they touch as long our people meet at the well.

Papa, Palti, and David, their lives and mine you'll share if you search these fragments. You've not heard of Palti? He's as real as Papa and David, as important to me, for good or bad, the great ones included me, a woman, gave a portion of their lives, withheld some of the best ... shared enough to make me want more, then shattered the vessel into a thousand pieces, and I went into a cave to mourn, when retching was done, came out to live on of a sort. I loved all three, I thought.

Wait, Palti shouldn't be in that list, he wasn't a king. But for his memory, men would be in the category of wolves and my life bitter. *But Palti is in my heart*, though I was shuffled about as a pawn, taken from one and given to another, once, twice. May God forgive my weakness.

My life is an old battlefield, a different spear hold ... and true, as my memory goes, good enough in the main, though I am weary. Check the record if you doubt.

Oh, it was worth living and telling about. If you're interested, open and explore, compare with what you know from hearing tales as water weeps from skins as it is carried. If you are a male, ask a female who goes to the well, usually they have no hesitation in sharing truth as well as gossip. If bits vary, give me a mustard seed of leeway – it's been a long time, storms cloud this mind, eyes and spirit nearly gone.

Hear my words, go to the record, see my heart and yours, where do they lead you? Can you hear me above the din of children, dogs, and servants? They have no concern of how they sound ... oh, aches weep as the water bag, from these hoary years.

Would you hear more of these groans?

"Oh, here you are, David, where have you been, I've been waiting ... oh, no, you're not David, why have you come here bothering me?" ... What was I saying, something about the early years? Come back tomorrow, I'll be rested then and we can continue our remembering.

God's care friend.
MICHAL'

CHAPTER I
PAPA SAUL AND I

   Little is changed in Israel after two kings flung their spears at life. Crickets rasp, birds sing, clouds pass over, breezes rustle grain-stalks, renew tired souls.
   The sun rises, awakens the jackal and vulture, the song bird warms hearts as men play their games at life: warring, ravaging, loving, planting and harvesting, building dreams while women tend the hearth: cooking, cleaning, bearing children ... some wondering about life and God ... and the sun goes down.
   Wonder spawns dreams, creates dancing rainbows in imagination; a rainbow may change a lifetime – leavening joy and sadness thereafter.
   I am one who wondered ... and, yes, joy and sadness leavened this life, that's right, both, Papa Saul favored me, encouraged a dream, put me into the face of Israel with his friendship, then gave me what I wanted: *David,* from that day faces changed with seasons, summer and winter lost distinction – sometimes warm winter, cold summer hammered as a flour pestle on stone.
   David warmed my heart, shared with me more than the others, caught me up in excitement, we loved each other, David and I ... *and I never knew him,* though I will tell you here that I did.

   Little changes in Israel, two kings flung their spears, talked to God, loved profusely, sang worship songs, a third went beyond them ... still, women tend the hearth, love, bear children – the lucky ones ... some wonder.

   I looked at papa in disbelief, he stood head thrust forward, eyes steely, neck tense, all the great bulk of him upset at me, in waves his emotion washed over me; face flushed, lips tight, searching for words, strain dominated papa's face as he delivered the ultimatum, *"You go to Palti of Gallim!"*

Words fell apart, my tongue clicked dry chaff; finally, *"Papa, you can't, I won't go!"*

"What do you mean, you'll 'not go?' I didn't ask, that is an order, it will be tomorrow at dawn! If you doubt, look at these soldiers who will accompany you, not only will they see you at daybreak, they'll see you through the night lest you flee, you'll go, Michal', oh, yes! you will go!"

Is this my loving papa speaking? I could feel my tongue swelling, words fell over themselves, when they came, it was, "Yes, papa," as a crumbling heart crashed about inside me. Thoughts darted about, searching something to divert him, to return him to the closeness we shared as I grew up worshipping him, then I wouldn't have dreamed of opposing kind papa, how could this happen? It isn't possible!

I looked at mama; she ignored me; Jonathan's eyes carefully shifted away; astonished dismay seized me at his easy defection, my playmate, my friend, but he did, he deserted me in my need, I would have fallen, except their several eyes propped me up, held me in place as an over-worn stiff garment. At once I felt alone, undressed, staked out in plain view, wishing to cover my body, my heart ... sensing arms twitching, yet no movement except the pounding in my chest.

My head slumped as the stomach knot swelled, quickly encompassed this body with aching numbness, become a whole-body worm contorting within and without. Papa doesn't understand, if he did, he'd comfort me with his big arms, great heart, call me sweet names of childhood, there is the cause, he doesn't understand, how could he know my need, when the wars of Israel pull him.

I should have known – Jonathan, mama, upset by papa's troubles, pulled by state uncertainties – at the river of life washing their own linen. I could blame it all on David, and partly it would be so; but even before David, turmoil seeds blew, scattered in tribal winds, entered garden walls of our Saul-spawned minds, took root there to become heart thorn bushes.

In remembering, I pause ... recalled hurts swell into new pain.

But surely, you, too, have known pain; we have something in common, you and I ... what? We have a common father somewhere, if I didn't feel that, you would not be hearing this voice, so long after. Traveling alone is lonesome, even with distance between us, your presence comforts me.

I can continue, though with pain ... we have only lives swirling in papa's emotional fields, now on the surface to be peppered by hail stones from his storm clouds, each of us seeking cover in any mind cave or crevice.

If that appears unsettled, it is no more than our family; first, unprepared papa was chosen king, probably because of his size, great presence. By our time, already he showed strain from responsibilities beyond his experience, pressures released with one away from mama ... God of our fathers, forgive me for disloyalty ... oh, that was long ago.

Within, I shouted, *"You can't do this to me, papa,"* ... afraid to tremble, realizing the danger was his state of mind, stress feeding fresh anger, fortunately, numbness bound me as a wrapped blanket, if opposing whimper had come, he would have lunged with his spear. *You think I exaggerate, he would not do that to his daughter? You may change your mind about that,* sluggish in fear, I would have been easy prey; anyway, he was twice my size, in his crisis, had he killed me, *it was his to do, my papa, my king.* Though surely he would come to himself before that.

We were at odds, who had been so close, and he ruled without outward resistance. I so easily defeated, with whom he shared plans as with no other except Jonathan, I, once allowed to chide him, his favorite. Has he lost his mind, have I?

How did we come to this disagreement, where was David while this went on? You will see.

You may come along as we retrace this journey, some I will tell, some as through other voices that we knew; much is recorded if you know where to look. There are those alive still who shared portions. If you doubt; no, even if you wonder, *go to them, you'll get as many versions as persons you ask* ... even so, you'll find colors true, facts are recorded. My views are mine alone, and, no other has gone through life with papa Saul, Palti, David, Jonathan, mama, outlived all of them ... without them, life loses the luster that makes it worthwhile, almost I would have them back, if it were possible.

Our trail climbs mountains, finds valleys, reopens Israel's hearth and soul – likely, not here soon again. You will see my heart as no other, neither papa Saul, nor David, oh, possibly one – you will know him well, even intimately, every one you will hear as I heard them, *my aged heart speaks! You are the first since one to see this mind....*

There will not be another like papa Saul, or David, history will hear these words because of them; also, of who speaks – only I have known all these so well. Who would you have tell the story?

One thing more, other light can shine on king-shaped history; adulation of these new kings dazzles Israel's memory, glosses over their excesses, accepts their versions. One who was of the household of both can peel the fruit, expose health and blemish, leaving naked pulp. Will you give me lodging while we view great and common events without the halo? If not, we must part, for this story will be told as known to me.

Does my name ring a bell? It should, I was along in Israel's great adventures ... I am a stranger to you? So be it, then let's share about this one that was.

Michal' is not a common name for a woman, King Saul has not told of its origins – as you know, he was my father. (Would I have chosen him? I'll think that over – *need I say, I loved him–I said it before? Remember that, my love for papa*, as our lives are pulled apart and up for review.)

Apparently I am, *or was*, physically attractive. Why would that be significant? It likely had much to do with twisting this fragile strand, because when David saw me, he was infatuated, I barely beyond childhood – not his only infatuation by far. This simple clue is a gossamer web ... floating, overshadowing the present and future of our lives, it hints to many things, foreshadowing nuances in David's character. *If only I could have read the pattern of those wispy fragments – it could have changed my life, but it wouldn't have, because, as with so many others, I would have seen only the halo adulation wove around beautiful David.*

My eyes, too, were blinded by the misty glow radiating from youthful David like shining hair on a sunlit head, no, more like the light from a great camp fire, undulating, flowing, flaming to every corner of the king's household, even to the nation.

This was the simple youth from the shepherd hills ... conflicting statements? Not at all; David was all of those, and more, where have you been if you don't know that?

All eyes turned to him, entranced by this unassuming, clear-eyed boy-man, playing and singing his way into our hearts. Beauty surrounded his form, echoing sweetly from the lyre strings vibrating from his carefully tuned soul, became one with his voice, entranced every maid within hearing, except one. How could even one remain aloof from this boy-man?

He made two heralded entrances to Saul's household, each spectacular, each widely different from the other, so distinct that one David seemed not to know the other. Am I confused? Possibly – probably. You will determine that as you follow my story, so deeply interwoven with those around us.

The handsome young man came walking to the king's court, accompanied by the messenger sent by papa to fetch him, his lyre cradled under one arm, tunic covering his sun-browned, sinewy body and upper legs; his sandals pushing out puffs of dust at every step in the heat.

His eyes took in this new territory with interest, noting the tense scrutiny pointed his way from scattered observers. Without apparent thought, the lyre was shifted into the playing cradle as soft notes of a tune drifted to the ears of the watchers – quickly enthralled listeners. Almost imperceptibly, the tension eased as the notes continued.

"What is the tune you play, shepherd?"

"It is one of my making; one that came to me through the baaing of lambs on a summer evening as I rested from bringing in a lost one ... I was at peace, it came out in the song."

"Why do you play it now?"

"I am tense as we near Saul's abode, I noticed those watching were as tight as I, it came naturally to ease them and myself with gentle music. It helped me, as it calmed the sheep, and appears to have relaxed these, the lyre strings are my path to inner peace."

"You may have more difficulty easing King Saul's tensions. At times he appears demented."

"Tell me about him, is there anything I should know that would help me serve him?"

"I would tell you to run and not return, except that would not solve our problem ... now I'm frightened, if you report my words, I'm done for."

"Have no fear of that, soldier, you've been a fair companion the whole of this journey, unless, of course, you display treachery, the king is God's choice and must be treated so."

"We'll move along, shepherd musician. If we take longer than the king thinks needed, we'll bear his displeasure, I desire none of that."

"We pick up the pace, then, there is no reason to anger the great one needlessly."

The puffs of dust quickened and continued until they came in sight of the compound. Quickly they were passed through the guards into Saul's presence, surrounded by the constant retinue.

As they entered the king's chambers, David once again gently picking the tune of the lost sheep that was found ... a hush of amazement gripped the assembly around King Saul; what effrontery this lowly shepherd exhibited, offering no bowing obeisance to the king. He continued playing softly as Saul's face took on the amazement of those around him, until Saul interrupted with a request, the same one others asked, "Tell me about your song, shepherd, it quiets my spirit."

"It is one I use when at peace, sometimes I tell the story that brought it to my harp. It is just beginning; I call it 'My Shepherd.' Each day, some bit is added, a portion of my life."

"You please me, shepherd musician, why have I not heard you before?"

"My years have been with sheep until recently, few other than sheep have heard this lyre. Loneliness of the pasture invades my music, loneliness from my life, through it I share with others, though mostly accompanying baaing sheep. Somehow the flock finds peace with it, as I, in times of storm, especially then."

"You shall remain here to soothe my torment, God speaks to me through your voice and strings."

"Who will tend my father's sheep?"

"Have you no brothers? I will send one without song to replace you."

As quickly as that, he was Saul's personal musician, constantly at his side, except as he returned periodically to tend his father's sheep, really, more to be away from papa Saul.

That was the first time the court saw David, those who watched carefully, saw his jaw twitch as he talked to Saul, casting doubt on his claim of peace, his air of simplicity ... too, it revealed his brotherhood with the rest of us as he faced King Saul.

Saul apparently missed it, I saw it from hiding but attached no significance to it at the time, spellbound as others by this winsome boy-man.

Why do you not hear the word love, did not everyone love David? For several reasons: David himself is one, he enchants an audience, women claim love; but there is a larger, more involved story, surely you've heard some of it, most have; however, many seem not to recognize the turns and sweep of David's personality, even in his later years. Or was it always there inside but hidden until opportunities were presented?

Do you know David well? Many *profess* to know him – are you one of those? And many of those see only one side of him, *a real one, certainly, but not the only person in David. Often I've wondered if always it was so with him from childhood.*

Possibly after much remembering and musing, we both will know him better as we scratch these memories. Don't let me influence you too much, *remember, the bias of my cloth is warped by experiences and years you don't know, scarred by abrasions from those close to me.*

At this moment, my thoughts of David are mixed, as with memories of papa, there are good and terrible memories of him –

none foreseen at mate bargaining, probably not considered in any event.

The halo of his comeliness was a shield off which negative perceptions ricocheted in early years, even for me, especially for me. For many, the halo served to the end, even against the assault of his later excesses ... already the shadow of my years with him is showing, a shadow partly of my own making.

Men may have been envious of him, of me, women, also, but only if they could not claim him, far too many did.

Our *affair*, David's and mine, was a mixture: first warmed with life, then cold to the marrow of the bone, still overpowering even in the worst of times. I speak for myself, of course; yet for David, too, unless every emotion he expressed was false – and that is not possible from the man we know. There, it is admitted again, David's beauty overcomes me even in distant memory. A man beautiful? In every way, including spirit.

Would I live it again if given the choice? *Likely* ... no, certainly; if I, who have seen so much of him, am so entwined, it's no wonder others, too, see only his halo.

You see, even in me the David halo survives. Who has been closer to him, seen more of his and life's patterns, what woman since Eve has had greater opportunity to influence the course of life? Both she and I missed opportunities, yet we were there....

What is this word *"affair"*? You will decide that as you know more of our story.

"Affair" may attach to generous portions of life – as, say, a long piece, a narrative. In my case, it was never far removed even when not uppermost, even when interrupted by David's running years, without me, when he could have had me with him, had he tried, he had others ... I cannot leave it!

Another reason? Because to me now, love has little to do with this life. (*Do I understand the word "love"?*)

Why should that surprise you, have you seen so little of our world? It has not changed that much since the times I tell about, may be long in changing. The David line is great, may for long change humankind with its extravagances, its worship; a paradox? We will see.

Have I always been disillusioned? Not always, and not more than other women, we have reason. As early as I can remember, it was clear who ruled, where plans were made, everything centered around men, they were important, women were about to keep the household functioning, which they did. One other duty was significant: to produce boys for the pride of the fathers – in the process to care for their never ending needs, a not unpleasant task, in the best of circumstances. Sharing that responsibility has its good and bad sides.

You see I understand life's patterns, where I fit in the scheme of things, does that contradict my denial of disillusionment, or add to it? How many sides have I?

For that matter, there is little to suggest women serve a purpose other than to please men, again, it is not an unpleasant role if executed with imagination, though needing appreciation to lift it a level. Most women do well with it as have I in the main.

Have I offended you, does this sound self-serving? Follow me, we'll see.

Papa was a large man, a head taller than other Benjamites, with big hands, great body and massive arms matted with dark hair to match his beard; handsome, attractive to women, awing to men, they saw him differently than we of course, we were accustomed to his size and presence; awed, but not to the same degree, sometimes the opposite.

Always in public his head was high, movements sure and strong. His decisions exuded confidence ... as much when wrong. Like David he controlled any show of insecurity – *almost always,* or should we be comparing David to papa? They were equally compelling, though in different ways.

Even in anger or madness he scattered decisiveness in all directions, littering landscapes with bodies and spirits for anyone within shattering distance, often those he loved most. His last landscape gathered into one the embittered frustrations of greatness gone sour, sadly pitiful.

That becomes more evident as events stack one on another, eventually revealing a pattern. How God appraised it, I don't know; seldom has he spoken to me; though whispers come from somewhere, if it is God, it would help if he would speak at least as strongly as did papa. On the other hand, he may not have so as not to allow papa to appear to be mirroring God, or, possibly God doesn't need the flowing emphasis to bolster an uncertain spirit, as did papa.

God's appraisal? We, his children, ponder that continually, likely as a means of appraising our own doings in relation to our understanding of God's wishes, or to align God to match our doings. Would we do that? How my thoughts fly in regard to that conjecture.

With arms raised for chopping thrusts, *"God told me to destroy them to the last child, the last sheep;"* ...there should be a word for that, for systematic killing of a people to the last child, not exterminate, *that is not expressive of the emotion brought up,* is it *herem*?

Papa was mesmerizing, hypnotic, equally with soldiers, women, his own children. Yes, I can understand we needed such a one as our first king. But there was another side of him, too, you will see much of it; mama, for one, was immersed in that hypnotic web. Another mixed metaphor? Whatever; it was numbing, destroying, slowly or quickly, dragging as a waterlogged boat in a stormy sea; mama was mired in his molasses sea, treading at the survival level. Do you understand? As we move along, it will be clearer.

Fortunately, Merab and I did not come by papa's size; though I more than she, I was rather tall but not great of girth, Merab, older than I, more petite, to me seemed more beautiful. She appeared so transparent, uncomplicated, gentle in her warmth, adapting to whim as necessary.

(Was-am, time blends down and upstream as a river caught in Israel, eddying behind a great rock outcrop, churning curdled clusters as goats milk to suit its own caprice – ending a bubbling cauldron, except alternating cold and hot, some *am's* change with time to *were*, though, mixing is a way of life with me.)

"Papa struts and postures, but under that he is simple and loving, little sister."

I stomped like the child papa thought me, "He's not loving when

MICHAL'

he sends me to the sleep mat early. I'm taller than you, nearing puberty, can't he see that?"

"Yes, he can see that; ...you're his baby girl, Michal'."

"You're the one he babies, he expects me to be adult except at bedtime, then I'm too young to see what goes on with the family, the mat will be a prison as long as papa rules my life."

"Maybe even beyond that, enjoy while you can, sister, it isn't all bad, getting away may not be what you think ... watch mama." There was a look in her eye I didn't understand.

"Why? She is dull, it's no wonder papa goes to another...."

"Hold your tongue, Michal', mama will hear you."

"Long has she known; why should we play silly games?"

"Is it silly to avoid taunting her with it? Besides, you called her dull."

"You're being dull, too."

"What you need is company."

"We have all the company we need, more than."

"You need more than your dolls, a dog?"

"I don't like dogs, their constant yipping upsets me; besides, the home is overrun with dogs."

In many ways we were opposites – she with a different body, eyes, a different mind; so simple and open in play, love, thinking of others' feelings more than her own. Am I without feelings for others? Certainly not, though likely not foremost as sometimes it is with her.

Was I telling about papa? It all goes together. The tales of our people speak mainly of heroes. How misleading; if it were not for their women, there would be no tales, or heroes.

You think I speak only of the physical part we play, the children we bear? Much more, the weave of our cloth is as complicated as the most intricate blanket design. Look closely, for without this, the nest is not tolerable, the mind expands the soul; yes, women have minds and souls. Too often, they are not given credit that way, it is sad that little things, even the package, so strongly influence others' thoughts about us. Foolish perceptions squeeze us into responses not our own choosing, often for which we are not fitted, I am not the person seen through this face and body, sometimes not even as seen through my words ... or am I mistaken once more?

What made life so complex, what is this mixture called Israel? Have only the men made Israel; have women not been involved? They think they've shaped us and it into their mold; largely they have ... certainly they control our lives, mostly because we're submissive, willing to accept men's dominance, to believe the legend they tell of their great wisdom – and allow them to set our paths, does God give them those privileges? It appears that will not change, our opportunities come through subtlety that influences them, not with strength. In that, you and I, are equal, if I'm speaking to females ... possibly, males, also, if you give me a bit of room.

Are you aware of Israeli heritage? Do you know how we got to this pass?

We'll not spend long telling, yet, you must know some if you are to feel the thrust of swords, the power of words; they swing about as chimes in gentle breezes, quickly changing to clashing swords in the tumultuous storms of our wandering. Weave those threads into a great blanket, cast it over Israel, draw it tight, and you have our scattered history often torn and ragged, under where falcon and vulture circle.

Our people came out of bondage in Egypt long ago. The story of the Exodus itself is a powerful tale of slaves, our people – Israeli slaves, led away from the slave-holders by a man called of God for a special need.

Since then, however, we have intermittently warred to occupy the land God brought us to through Moses, Aaron, and Joshua. Never for long have we known peace, *you would think it would have been better with God as our king* – speaking through priests and prophets, of course. (He, God, might have trusted us with a bit of direct speaking, oh, well.)

Even with that, our lives are sweet except for constant torment of the Philistine barbarians, always our guards are alert, watching for swift assaults from the wilderness; rarely do they get to us without encountering our men; they shouldn't, with God's protection, but sometimes they do. It may always be so.

That is what brought papa to power. That what? The never-ceasing barbarian attacks, *of course,* and the corruption among Samuel's sons whom he'd made judges.

(*The holy man tolerated that, thereby possibly limiting his own power. Over and over, men prove their humanity, including holy men and kings, though we dislike to believe that.* Why doesn't God choose better? I've wondered about that, too, possibly he makes do with those at hand, stirring the pot to allow the best to surface before lifting out his choice, and the rest of us remain to question, even when we should trust.)

Until papa became king, they – the Philistines – won more battles from our armies than they lost; *yes, with God as our commander often we lost,* you know what that did to us.

Always we were either under attack or under their heels, wondering why God allowed it. Neither was comfortable; our questioning – wondering about God's whereabouts made it worse, as God punished us for disobedience.

Not that Philistines didn't have provocation for killing our children ... under '*herem*', holy war, our warriors did their best to destroy enemies to the last child, when we invaded Philistia – as did the Philistines when they came on us. *You will see, oh, yes, you will see.* (Consider David's training missions with his army of six hundred, while he was running from papa. David's plan during those forays was *to kill every witness, he nearly succeeded.* We'll speak more about that later when we talk about papa's warring and disobedience – *he called it obedience.*)

Too many losses and Philistine domination eventually caused our people to demand a king to unite Israeli tribes for better defenses; Samuel resented that, understandable as it is to us.

What people can tend flocks or till the soil when constantly afraid of enemy attack, could you? It is done with great difficulty, furrows wobble; men workers, women, too, watch brush and trees instead of oxen or sheep, startle at a sudden noise or movement is normal. You don't come up behind a wary tiller of soil or shepherd without notice.

Eventually, our people grew weary of life under threat of attack, grumbled, asked God's spokesmen for better leaders. *Eventually?* Sooner than that, but answers didn't come at once.

Samuel did better for a while but not good enough, worsening as he grew old, allowing free rein to his corrupt sons whom he had appointed judges. Our people saw the sons as an extension of God's rule, putting doubt on God as well as Samuel, that, too, may have caused God to spank us in spirit. Why us? Can't you see? The leaders we follow cut our swath and we are at fault ... history tells us that, so does God.

When leaders from the twelve tribes came to Samuel with petitions for a king, Samuel saw that as rejecting himself, did what any leader would do: *Knowing it would change his role considerably, Samuel did his best to convince them of their error.* He told them, your king will ... "take your sons and appoint them to his chariots and to be his horsemen, and to run before his chariots; and ... some to plow his ground and to reap his harvest, and to make implements of war ... your daughters to be perfumers and cooks and bakers. He will take the best of your fields and vineyards and olive orchards and give them to his servants ... and you shall be his slaves...."

They refused to listen to Samuel's remonstrance; demanded a king to be like other nations. You could hear all this from any Israeli man or woman – warrior, shepherd, tiller of soil, or woman at the well – she, better informed than most men.

It began far back, as our people grew restless with God's leadership interpreted by priests and prophets; good men, great men, but men – every one fallible, liable to err unless God removes their right of choice. God shielded Samuel by taking blame when Samuel felt personal affront as the tribes demanded a king.

Did God do Samuel a favor not to call attention to his wink at wormy corruption in his own family, they who served as spokesmen for God's rule? *But possibly he did call attention to it and we were not told,* it is not God who recounts these happenings. Or is it God, through His own means?

It took a fateful turn when papa was selected for his role; quite another when David replaced him – as different as could be, it will not be difficult to see the changes.

"Where is he?" called Samuel, swinging his hoary head about to

give emphasis to the question – heard by the assemblage gathered to hear God's choice, *"Where is the one selected by God to be our king?"* Un-king-like papa skulked in the baggage; yes, that great body skulked, step by step Samuel's hunt progressed to the great young man found in the baggage.

It's quite a story, often told by papa and then by others, fortunately, most have heard it. This episode illustrates the humanity of great leaders, so called.

David's entrance to Israeli history was more spectacular and longer heralded, needing no telling by David to spread the story. That, too, likely was included in papa's jealousy that steadily increased his madness. Who, even you, could stand to see a shepherd take over your domain, your flock, your hard-won territory? With territory goes household, harem, family loyalty ... there it becomes absolutely personal!

Was that too brief? We'll fill in gaps as we go along.

Why was I chosen to be caught in the twist of Israel's rough garment? Some would say it was the fate of the gods; there's a kernel in that, one that bears more thought ... but our God is more involved, *more personal sometimes.* (Watch for that, too, as we continue.)

Evidently, when I slyly made myself visible to David, he liked what he saw, in any event he was not overly wroth when papa doublecrossed him and gave Merab to Adriel of Meholah for wife. David's lack of anger confused papa at the time, confused everyone, actually. Would you like to know my thoughts at the time? *Let's hold that, they become visible as we go on, already, you may have surmised the answer, though there is more to it than that.*

Then it was – in that small woman Merab – we saw a sleeping giant, greater than Goliath, David, any that followed. Everyone knew sweet, transparent Merab; in a moment, no one knew Merab, transparent no longer, no longer the clear glass, at the least smoky.

Adriel of Meholah? You don't know where Meholah is? It doesn't matter, we didn't either ... it must have been important to papa.

I see, you become impatient with this wandering; it's no wonder.

My mind drifts with dry balsam leaves among vagrant memory winds, one sighing to another, and yet another, as still another answers. My mind is a hummingbird catching, dropping the vanished fragrance, sometimes nectar, other times bile; then it becomes a mockingbird injecting useless thoughts. God planted my memories, lifted by soft winds, hurricane winds, turbulent winds, watered them with rippling rivulets and roaring floods; each touched my spirit with its flavor, delicate fragrance, crashing cymbals, you are seeing the fruit of that planting.

Our lives would have been so simple had papa not become king. Likely most of the chaos in his personality wouldn't have happened, possibly, he could have been the uncomplicated papa-hero of our childhood imaginations, except for certain traits that were part of his being.

Mama might have continued her fantasy of papa's affection – *might have, but not necessarily.* The chaos is one knob, on papa's mind that well may have come forth with him from the womb, seeing him now, it's difficult to imagine him making the usual entry into life, though likely he did.

Even without kingship, papa's handsome presence would not have been isolated from the woman-lure strewn about with his innate scent; certainly he had *that* long before being tapped by Samuel. Such is not always a blessing, though much envied by men, sought by women. There is much talk but little respect for fidelity among Israeli men, probably others as well – a bias based on observation and family experience, and broader. It sounds as though God does not approve of infidelity, though His disapproval does not appear to divert the stream of disobedience.

Papa was a local leader already, but who would have dreamed he would become king of all Israel? Not even papa saw that possibility; or did he? Certainly he didn't.

Until then, God was our king, that should have been adequate for our people – Benjamites and the other tribes. *Of course it was not.* But, I've said that, haven't I?

Don't be churlish, we are getting to the point.

MICHAL'

"Michal', you should have been a boy, with your interest in war strategy and men's doings, I could have made a great general of you, possibly a great king; but that is foolish thinking; you're a girl and will remain so."

"I like being your girl, papa, though your stories put my thoughts with the army. No, no, I would not be a man, papa, what makes you say such a thing?"

And I would not, yet somewhat I believe him, to this day.

That doesn't imply what you may think, physically and mentally I am a woman, as a child it was easy to fall into feminine routines of a well-off tribal leader, become king, not the simple man he sometimes claimed, though never seriously.

Papa had other women than mama – concubines, one whom we came to know (you heard right), and friends. Being the wife, mama was the household manager, early we realized that didn't mean she was the favorite. At the time we thought little about where papa spent his waking sleep hours, we were accustomed to his absences. That doesn't mean we didn't know.

"After supping will you tell us stories about when you became king, papa?"

Wiping his mouth with his arm, "I have duties this evening. Some time soon, I will."

"Don't wipe on your arm, it mats your hair disgustingly! Would it hurt you to take an evening from shadow activities to be with your own children?"

"Tend your responsibilities, woman, I have things to do that are none of your affair. What do you mean, '*your own children*?'"

"What is this great '*affair*' not my concern? Are you planning another war with the Philistines? Have you entered into negotiations for new territory, a meeting with your great generals, *or have you discovered a plump new fig to taste? Have you forgotten that you have children?*"

"I go to Samuel to offer sacrifices and to get direction for the next campaign ... what if I *have* discovered a new fig to enjoy? You asked ... it is so! Why would you bring it to our children, have you no shame? Where are my children?"

"Who speaks of shame? Where is your sense of proportion? Your children have minds and ears, they understand your heart is not here, or your children."

"Worse and worse it grows, your carping and complaining never ends, what did I see in you?"

"Whatever it was, you had it quickly and turned to others."

"Woman, you have no modesty!"

"You left me none, *oh, great one*."

And so it was, women and neglect, neglect for our mama.

We hurt with her. As always, papa won, though not always with the last word, as you heard.

Mama's figure drooped momentarily, then her head came up as she surveyed her household – a small queendom, but adequate, only under papa's rarely flaunted neglect did her courage falter. I said *small* ... only in comparison to papa's kingdom. It was a large household, within many rooms, many persons, none in Israel was larger. Later, there were several larger, much larger, extending to many households; David's and Solomon's among them. Nevertheless, papa dignified the practice – observed by many, envied, and followed by David and Solomon and most wealthy Israelites. (Is dignified the right word?)

Have we lost our thought about households? Somehow it has encompassed our problems of fidelity and the growth of harems, what flows from them, affecting individuals, families, nations? How God viewed this I do not know, within this is wrapped some of my continuing confusion; a different mind might have accepted and adjusted, or numbed; I did neither.

Papa's wandering did not affect his attentions to us despite her words. When not on campaigns, he was careful to share time with us, if not mama intentionally. Like it or not, some of his attention went to her by default, not well used by her when it came, she seemed not able to hold her tongue when it would have served her better.

Being children of the lawful wife gave us status and privileges, being a girl, the second at that, subtracted a few points, though enough remained to enjoy, during childhood years it was adequate.

Merab and I should have been reversed, or Jonathan and I. Neither of them made the most of their lives. Amend that ... in their own ways they did, in time I appreciated both; always we got along well, almost always; how lonely it is without them.

Children of concubines did not fare as well, they of the same lineage, yet not. Here is an example of the male's singular place in life, extending to the mists of antiquity, likely into mists of the future, as well. It was odd – everyone, including mama, knew the situation, that papa shared other women's beds, other children were of his seed. In official company it was never mentioned; seed, tares, wheat scattered by the winds – mostly as little considered in their survival, these children of Saul.

How much credit does God get for that? Men would give him much; you don't understand? What can I say? Men expect women and God to accept their wandering fidelity, a departure from holiness; families, women, sacrificed to male slippery minds, surprisingly some do accept it, women, that is; I wonder, would God?

If so, women have reason to ask, "Why, God?" Have they questions about God's winds in their balance of seasons – as humans of great or little value except to catch and harbor scattered seeds? In seasons of the soul, crying of the heart.

And the scattered tares, those created and diminished by men's needs, what are their questions, are they not children of God, also? Even if not claimed by the father?

Had papa acknowledged them by marrying his concubine, they would have been our equals; without that they lived in limbo – a place or state of oblivion just outside hell with little chance of earth's heaven – shared his love but not other privileges, deprived of all but dreams.

Later, the dreams, too, were taken from them on the whim of another – all determined by who their father was, they without benefit of privileges. You will attach to this again later.

Why did he not grant them that easy to give opportunity of acceptance, especially since his attentions went to their mother? Obviously, he loved them.

I do not know; he never said; now I wish I'd asked. His answer may have been the same as another time when he accused me of prying; in that he revealed the precipice so near my innocent but questioning walk.

As much as they would allow, we dominated them, as children, and then as adults. You would know who they are? Some in due time; others likely we did not know. It was not mama's affair; it was not our affair until it became so, I was the one eventually most affected.

How was it in our household? We had three, no, four separate sharing-units among the king's offspring – of the kings-line, that is, you will see how important that was over the span of years.

Jonathan often was alone with papa because as first son he would be king after papa. Special grooming for future responsibility came with that; everyone assumed he loved his place and potential.

Jonathan and I went off alone to let down our defenses, oh, yes, we built defenses and escapes very young, because of those close times sometimes I expected more of him than he was prepared to give. Already you've seen one instance of that, later, when David who could have been a threat to him was involved with us, Jonathan's commitment extended much further. That causes much wonderment in my remembrance of him.

You soon learn that life in the king's court is a game played always at high tempo basted with intrigue, eventually lacing into family groupings, each seeking advantage. Children of the king gained both protection and danger – the danger carried various odors, of words, or swords – the last less imminent but as real, very real; certain for some of the king's clan, none escaped entirely. *You will see this is not fantasy, how real it became as years accumulated!*

Papa, himself, was peppered liberally among the dangers, time will verify these to you. You will agree that *'pepper'* does not do justice to the condition described, he was never innocuous as a condiment or sneeze, as some sneezes are explosive as wheat-dust ignited by 'sparks from the eye of the devil, a phenomenon seen seldom, fortunately, but seen. There were later times when papa and the devil were intermixed in my mind – but that is ahead of our story again.

In our own family, the tug between mama and papa harried us, pulled us apart as a cooked fowl being divided, other pulling was as constant, worrying us as a dog on its bone. One finds ways of getting free of it when possible.

Other times it was Merab and I pairing off, as we were not allowed into men's doings – at that time, boys' and men's doings, the mysterious cult ruled by virtue of physical structure – type and position. Some have the important appendage, some don't.

My pique is showing, isn't it, what a world we live in; how did God think up the categories and privileges of life? How does he decide who gets the benefits and who gives them? Who gets which structure? Those who could ask God either did not or did not report the reply.

Another grouping was the three other brothers, Malchishua, Abinadab, and Ishvi – sometimes called Ishbosheth; and sometimes it was Ishvi going alone, with his ambitions, then probably only dreams – briefly coming to fruit after papa's death, later proving to be his end and those who aided him. That is another story worth telling, sometime … too many a-building. We'll see how that goes.

Is that five? It takes the appearance of a snake den, so intermingled one wonders how they untie to depart the den. Snakes? Considering the snake den, untie they must; I have never heard of them rotting in a pile, although their odor would leave that impression. It comes as easily to our brood of Benjamites, changing alliances between units from one time to another … often, though not always, with the odor of the snake den.

Odd how a man's household swings and rattles in the winds moving about his position in life, sometimes gentle, as often violent, alliances thought to be permanent, suddenly shift, creating lasting enmities, deaths, new alliances, new intrigues, new enmities. Do you see what it did to us? Do you understand our identity, our similarity with yourself?

How different it would have been had Samuel not heard God's instruction to anoint papa; if he had decided it was a sour-stomach dream – of course he heard God as God intended.

These alliances or misalliances you will observe as scenes change, often with pain to someone or several; remember this thought as you see our often stupid, even painful stumbling – in some instances far beyond boundaries of convention even for kings.

So many things we did revolved around our religion, *to us it was more than serious business, it was our way of thinking, often carried to extremes*. When I told you God was our king, *it was that way!* Some would call us religious fanatics, sometimes we were, as you'll see from time to time; a fanatic is one with ways that differ from or exceed another's custom.

Naturally God spoke to us through judges and priests as His interpreters, Samuel was the greatest with his aura of authority, when he stood before us trumpeting out his conversations with God, we trembled; sometimes even papa did. Yes, papa trembled, but no one had courage to remark on it, certainly not I. Samuel surely saw it, tucked it into a crevice for sometime retrieval and use against papa. Mostly not even Samuel was so bold as to challenge papa in his furies.

Often Samuel spoke with papa in private; the only person who scolded papa with impunity, I came as near it as any other in the early days. Close as papa and brother Jonathan were, he never differed with papa in those years, later, as you will see, Jonathan's odd mind-bent slanted history as much as any valorous deed of war, then he came to odds with papa almost as much as I, sometimes maybe more.

Challenging or scolding papa? Walking into a field of broken glass or a river of crocodiles would be reasonable comparisons; then I knew, though at first I didn't fear him; early, he was kind to us – contrasting to later clashes with Merab and me, and others, too.

Merab clashed with papa, sweet Merab? Yes, sweet Merab finally rebelled.

As with mama, papa's roving independence brought him into conflict with Samuel's will. However, Samuel had residue authority from God to bolster his position and keep papa somewhat in check; whereas mama had no advocate, none at all except her wits and presence, which were considerable in her domain.

Papa often usurped God's authority, each time causing trouble between himself and Samuel. Several times, he heard, "What have you done this time to incur God's wrath, Saul? You can go too far, you know." The defiant answer was a cloak for a quickly hidden flinch, "I am king, holy man. God appointed me, and don't forget it."

Samuel was aware of his own part in causing that and was not to let papa forget that, either.

With our people it saved worry to believe God was in charge ... others made many decisions for us; that way we could concern ourselves with pleasing God as the '*holy ones*' encouraged; for both, letting them make our decisions and pleasing God, we were praised, and scolded when we fell short of praising God.

Even better was it when God went before us in battle, the Philistines found God more than they could chew, unfortunately, many times, even before papa became king, God was neglected or not informed of the danger. Many battles were won by the marauding invaders; sometimes after papa became king, too; some said God was dead when invaders reached us; others claimed He'd forgotten us. I never entered into that, it was beyond my field of knowledge, very far beyond.

We trembled and were proud when papa trumpeted, "God has assured me of his presence, those Philistines will not return to their hearths."

And many did not, many of our own as well – little was said of our losses, though, except for the wailing of their wives and children. Usually, before going into battle, papa told of God's going before our troops; in disaster, he licked his wounds and said nothing to his surviving men or their families. In war, men die, even in the presence of God; possibly a good place to die. Sometimes God seemed to have gone away, other times papa forgot to take God with him into battle – it appears God wants to be asked.

Always, though, God found it necessary to return to papa's assistance. I don't understand why he didn't allow papa to remove enemies permanently – possibly we needed to devote more time to pleasing God to get that blessing.

Or was there a limit to the killing, or was the killing not his choice? Papa would deny or avoid those as he did when I once questioned God's instructions to kill to the last woman and child – if heathen or not ... how could our men know? Do men always go to war wearing a symbol of faith, or heathen? Some do; are they always accurate, truthful, blessed of God, as they say?

We never had opportunity to ask these questions of Samuel,

likely, he would say, "It is none of your affair." We found that you do not question instructions from God, for one thing, it implies doubt of the messenger's truth or doubt that God sent the message – either way, it's dangerous ground. As yet, I've found no way to ask God directly about his instructions, evidently he does not wish to be troubled except by his anointed few.

Of course it isn't my affair. God has more important things for us to do.

You are becoming accustomed to these musings? That is good; I fear we're hung with them – as they say at the well....

Did I say God went before us? There I go including myself with warriors again. These many years after, emotionally I join their doings, in a way, it has worked to my gain, in that often they underestimate me, little realizing that sometimes my thoughts race ahead of theirs.

Men do that, they believe women are shaped only for certain activities, that they never think of other things ... men, those who know us so well, have some to learn about us – those who lay the cobblestones of our paths, or tell us to do so.

They like their biases; see women as wanting the same as they, in the main we may; though in the end the brightest of women use that to their advantage. Others you will see in our story have done more in that regard than I, too often I was caught and bound in my own emotions, built or encouraged by a man to whom I attached.

Am I too exclusive? Are there many like this, or am I an oddity? Papa saw something when he said, "Michal', God should have made you a boy." He may have wished because of our closeness at that time, later it was not so.

In some ways he showed so much insight; his many years as king attest to that. In ways he was stupid; but that was papa Saul, a mixture of mind, muscle, promiscuity, and insecurity – usually hidden behind bluster and arrogance. As you know, it finally caught him in a most painful manner. I see him bleeding on the ground with three of his sons dead around him.

Before that, however, his life showed signs of God's anointing, along with the insecurity and increasing madness; in those he proved himself human, as are we all.

Let's go back to the "promiscuity." That may be unfair to papa if compared to those who followed ... no, let's leave it there; comparison is not involved. He was not faithful to anyone except Jonathan.

I was fortunate to be produced from the legalized relationship; how important is a simple ceremony. Why did papa not call out divorce on mama and marry the one who claimed his affections? It would have been so easy, so simple – "I divorce you," and give her a bill of divorcement, in that, God's man Samuel might not have challenged him.

But I've forgotten or my emotions are directing my thoughts; God allows more than one wife. He could have married her any time he wanted, no one forces a man to give attentions to his wife or wives, more than he wishes, what punishment mama endured, without a blow marking her. But was it so simple? Six of us came from that union; the first seeds of his loins, we are evidence that, at least for a time, she attracted him.

Do I assume more than fact? Was she simply the available woman? Was he a celibate youth? Was he busy with others earlier than mama's last birthing? Questions without answers, to me, at least. (My mind plays tricks. Certainly he was busy earlier, our brothers of the love relationship attest to that, more often of late my mind does that.)

Answers to several of those I don't know, something restrained him from declaring divorce. Will we know better as we follow his whirling in the wind? Possibly.

Certainly he whirled in the wind, what else could account for his behavior? On occasion he soared as he whirled, almost as a drunken falcon.

As for the marriage, it is much more complicated than choosing between two women, papa did that, chose between them, when he set up the household of the other not a stone's throw from us, virtually a part of our household, thereby establishing a pattern for future kings, a practice to be emulated and expanded ... needing little encouragement or example.

That he did not bring her directly in speaks about his respect for or fear of mama – does fear cast the distinction? Possibly not, but akin to it; something held him from casting her out; possibly the fear of God, for God may have held her in more regard than papa did. On the other hand, she was a superb household manager, perhaps more valued than I realized.

At first, mama forbade us to cross that short distance. At first, we had no desire to do so.

We were ashamed for mama that he flaunted his illicit offspring. As with the numbness of a death in the family, eventually we grew tolerant and no longer noticed mama's pain, she, too, eventually flinched less, stoically accepting what was. Mama didn't smile often, neither was she grim – merely too occupied to be bothered with pleasures of children or foolish men. It puzzled me that she could be so engrossed in such banal activities, oblivious to exciting doings going on around her.

One day, I asked her, "How can you bury your nose in trivia when life is all about you, mama?"

"You have no idea what joy I find in what I do, daughter. This is not trivia. There may come a day when you will find jewels in common things as have I."

"I'll never let myself be buried in dull routines; you have opportunity to expand your life and you don't bother."

"Have I?"

Was she heavy, thin, tall, short? She was mama! Papa would be the only one interested in that, what male would have courage to more than glance at her? Probably, she was attractive, even beautiful once, now less so, heavier, paying less attention to it. Had she not been pleasing once, papa's interest would have been short; knowing papa, he had something to say about his mate, custom or no. If you doubt that last, consider the part some, both man and woman, have in the stories we yet share.

Or is my appraisal lacking depth? What attracts a man to a woman, a woman to a man? Seeing the pairings off of many, one's amazement is multiplied; opposites, handsome and plain, large and small, are as frequent ... but that is beside the point; most have no say in the matter. It may be as well, for one appears as content as another.

MICHAL'

In matter of fact, the unrecognized one in papa's affections was surprisingly plain; very slim, undeveloped in comparison to most mature women; she was quiet, but with a warm smile and pleasant way after one found her out. But we'll come back to her.

Mama bore me yet never shared my interests or understood my frequent, she said, "unpredictable turns." She can't be blamed for that, no one sees the mind of another, even a mother, though it is interesting to try – as now. I am thinking of yours as well as these we talk about. Though I don't know you, again I say, "We are much alike."

After papa and I prolonged a conversation, excluding the others even though surrounded by them, she scolded me with, "Why do you bother with men's things, daughter? They have only hurt for female children, God has not balanced things well in our world."

I looked up quickly, where had that originated in this woman who appeared bound by routine, uninterested in the excitement of life? Had papa missed something?

"Discussions like that will lead you nowhere but into disappointment. Women will not share that part of life."

"Papa is only talking out his plans to hear them, to catch flaws as he unfolds them before his own mind. It is exciting hearing them, have you never done that?"

"You are too young to put your mind into his world. It will take you into desires that will not be filled."

"I only listen to please him, mama."

Yet I dreamed of seeing them fulfilled, 'seeing' not doing. Honestly, though, I dreamed of being involved, joining in battle, even if it would not be. Could I have killed men, women? Maybe... . but little children? That is one of my problems, if God approves mass slaying of innocents, where is mercy? Help me with that if you can; tell me, I want to find where God is.

"*Honestly*," I said; if I am not honest, the whole of this is wasted. At this crossing in life, honesty is not the best policy, any other is wasted – largely so in earlier years, but not always.

Who understands another's mind? Seeing another's thoughts through completed acts helps, even then the pattern defies understanding, especially my acts – and Papa's too; lest we play favorites let's include David – he earned his place over the years. And what of mama? Where was she in all this? Merab more than any other, none in these ramblings fits a perfect pattern. No more does Israel, always, there is the hunger for God's direction; always there is misunderstanding or coming up short.

In some ways mama fared better than most, that which she needed to do she did; *she found her role as manager of the household and played it well.* No king ever was more dominating. In these matters papa saw her value, by default allowed her domestic power. Others allowed it because she assumed it, and papa did not countermand her often, if he had, she would have quit and he would have lost a valuable service, she would have lost a mind-saving vocation.

In kingdom affairs she had less influence than the other, in things of love, none at all. Sometimes I puzzle over the whimsies of shared intimacy gone by; it has become a habit of late, I've had time and occasion.

Finding ways around her sharpened my wits, sixteen years under her direction made me a skilled manipulator in some things as you will see. Others I never learned; possibly too interested in matters not open to me.

"Girls, go see to work in the cooking quarters. It will sharpen skills you will need sometime."

"I would have another lesson in marketing, mama, may I continue what was begun? It was of great interesting to me."

"Oh, of course, daughter, Merab will do cooking supervision."

Again I went to market with its bustle of activity, excitement, sweet and rotten odors mixing – become gross and attractive, sweat, animal and human filth, hacking of phlegm, droppings of animals, cacophonous hawking of merchandise, raucous bargaining, sudden agreement, exchange of coin and product, mysterious peoples from distant lands, thieves, anger, kindness when least expected. All as exciting to me as to you; you've seen it all.

I suspect she saw my manipulation and indulged it, sensing my need for freedom while there was yet time; of course, I believed myself the unsuspected director of important adventures.

MICHAL'

You think already the tale is told? It's barely begun, stay with me; you'll taste excitement that shaped kingdoms, in the tasting, you will notice the gentle and violent intermingling, sometimes to calm hearts to peace – *that gradually*, then again to tear them, leaving them to bleed – and those remaining never free of the same lurking possibility.

My life, like yours, had its share of both, fortunately; who would want sunshine without storm throughout every day of a lifetime, or eternity? Do I really mean that? I think so, though a bit more sunshine would have been acceptable.

In the early years, papa was busy with his obsessions: maintaining his kingdom, his women, and (should I say?) his God – constantly shifting attentions as his moods changed. Each powerful, dominating in its place and time, each finds portrayal in our tale.

At one time, mama imagined herself his one love. An illusion, I have concluded men are incapable of faithfulness, only one of their shortcomings, one of many, but the important one to women.

On the other hand, once a woman recognizes this, it is an aid in her coping scrambles, mama adjusted well after the first shock, though she was long in accepting it, if at all.

Every woman alive maneuvers, how she does that tells how well she lives. Here is more of my bias, resulting from years of isolation caused by bungled maneuvering; don't be impatient, you'll have opportunity to be lavishly impatient with my stupidity in due time.

With animated glow, mama included papa in her excitement in planning for the morrow's celebration, "We'll spread our lunch on the blanket. It will be a pleasure to share again with papa after his days of royal business."

"I'll not be with you, woman, Army problems call; you'll get along without my company."

"Saul, we count on you for a day together ... your own children need you."

"I said you will get along without me, woman."

Her face contorted as she ducked her head.

With clouded eyes, Papa looked away from her hurt ... womankind hurt, known by every female who tries to be something she cannot. I repeat, God made a few mistakes, placing women in second position was the most serious, we must find paths around that.

"Who is the woman among the officers, mama?"
"I don't know, child, likely an entertainer. Pay no attention to them."
"She is giving attention to papa, can't you see that, mama?"
"She is paying attention to him because he is King. Here, help with the cloth and food."

Again, it was so, either mama could not see, or wished not to, turned her back so not to be tempted to look. Obviously, papa chose to bring his fawning retinue within mama's sight to humiliate her for her recent outburst, mostly, he didn't put that on her, today his anger slopped over into our view, and our hurt.

Her defenses crumbled for a moment, you know how she twisted inside and out, once more her back stiffened as she turned away, she knew the situation, and only in surprise did her defenses fall briefly.

You continue to form opinions of me, already you see me as a strongminded female? How would you have me, soft, compliantly bending to the winds of men's desires? Life is sorted into categories by sex, *that is a fact learned by experience,* but to make pleasing men a vocation, to me is short of doing them justice. Always to get their wishes harms them, excess begets more excess; in the end all are harmed, once begun, by male or female, excesses multiply until nothing good remains.

When and where did I form that opinion? Watching and hearing papa taught me sometimes what not to do, besides, do you imagine me a sheltered soul never away from watchful eyes? Have I always been in the king's household, did I not say, *'This is many years later?'*

Have you traveled with an army, have you seen the slaughter, the ravaging of countryside and women, including girls, man's abusive use of any female at all?

What does it do to marauding victors? Are there no littered trails in their souls? – *Trails whose scars shine white and cold to the end of life, dragging hard over the lives they share in enemy and home country, it is not possible to live so and not be self inflicted.* We need not speak of God in this, we trample ourselves.

Am I weaving strangled dream-strands into soiled imaginary webs? Am I fantasizing the worst of men into all men? You may think that if you wish, if so, you are the one painting skewed dreams of reality.

Have they no families at home, is morality an illusion? Does it go on vacation only in war time? Is there reason to believe that even papa minded his manners when warring with heathen peoples? Oh, for conscience woven into living fabric. Did he, they, do so when at home among God's chosen, the civilized? Do what? Have we lost you with these musings?

But then, what are morals to a given person: king, soldier, or camp follower, even to you or me for that matter? Each person has a version to apply for convenience.

Papa, too? And Samuel? Certainly; what of Samuel's appointment of his sons to judgeships, and then his tolerance of their corruption? Usually ignored so as not to hurt his self-appointed 'holy' men! And who uses the camp followers, only a few wayward souls? That's not the word in these parts, *do you think there are no camp followers because of the rule that men shall be kept from women when at war? How naive to think it enforced in routine travels. Do the lust lives of their leaders bear that out?*

And when the victory's won, do the victors rape before slaughter? Too often have papa and David demonstrated otherwise ... read the lives of the leaders – when lust intervenes, any measure, forbidden or not, is undertaken with skill and cunning ... am I blaspheming our God-appointed leaders? Does it matter who appointed them if they sin? Surely, God does not look the other way when even heathen are violated.

Holy war? Does God involve himself in any of that? We are told he does. Sad thoughts are these, I am frightened and confused, searching for God. Yet, who that knows the chill drippings of war would doubt? I wish my infant fantasies of war without hurt could be true. Sometime civilized peoples will do better, possibly when they understand God better, possibly even to understand the hurt of a soul through the hurt of a body, woman or man.

What of the lives of those being used, in whatever manner, are they not persons? Including those who have the misfortune to be in the conqueror's path, whether called women or children?

If you listen to idle stories of men, these part-time soldiers, you will hear of excesses beyond belief, orgies that would not be tolerated except among conquered peoples who cannot protest. Restraints are forgotten; somehow in the process women are thought of as without feelings, without ability to hurt ... women of other nations and religions are without souls, in the view of conquerors.

Men squandering their manhood on groups of women or if only one is available at the moment, in single file on the same woman. You believe Israeli soldiers are immune from that joyous plunder, turned to obsessive gorging, insanity of a kind? Some boast of rejoining the file, awaiting another plundering satiation ... you think it idle talk? Then you do not face reality either, our Israeli men, too, are human, proved so again and again.

It is no wonder men join armies and face death, it must be sweet inducement indeed, considered from a man's viewpoint. What joy it must be to force oneself on a helpless female or several, even girls of nine or ten ... sweeter, juicier morsels.

Is the experience more pleasurable, does it increase the male's self image? Does it prove manhood to be the tenth or twentieth to dominate one who is seeking flight from reality, the only escape from a series of males tearing apart the mind of a human being?

God has no more to do with that than with *herem*, though both have been credited to Him. Surely, that is not why God is called "*Him*" ... God would not approve of such conduct. (I apologize to you for this outburst. God may not approve of this any more than of the actions spoken of. You, too, may reject these thoughts, but please see if there is any of God's intent in them before doing so, look for my heart in my words.)

Where do these thoughts take you? Is every girl a daughter, a sister, would you hurt for her, or toss her off with, "*Woman was made to pleasure man,*" whether Israeli or another? Is freedom from restraint that important? It appears so for many. Who wants compliant females? (We are back to that.) Half the population, apparently – with a few exceptions, of course.

Once more you question my acquaintance with reality, now perhaps you think me involved in excesses of imagination. If so, listen to these boasting soldiers yourself when they don't know you listen … or those used … with enough searching, a few of those used may be found who have returned to sanity – if our own soldiers have not in turn been defeated and our women and girls similarly treated, in that event, talk to our own.

The outburst is over for the moment; we will grant that not all men fit the pattern drawn here. Some are as fine gold to the innermost strand; however, it is not necessarily the ones so lauded by storytellers or popular word of mouth.

There, now, you've formed another impression of me based on my rambling, one that may or may not be accurate … again, hold judgement until you have further facts, they will be forthcoming as we journey along.

Life in a king's family has its tales. You thought the excitement was finished in the battlefield exploits, killing, marauding? If so, you mistake grandly. Since you have come this far, you may stay, though you may still withdraw … considering we are too plainspoken.

CHAPTER II
THE Fabric of a worn cloak
don't despair, colors revive.

We have been rubbing the fabric of a worn cloak, experiencing its shabbiness ... in me and as I knew it in others. Don't despair, the spirit revives, much of this life has been satisfying because of *good* thriving in the midst of *mal*, never is life all good or all evil ... almost never.

God speaks through heavy curtains sometimes, but He speaks, often goodness is most expressed without words in the lives of those least heralded, and other times great goodness lifts as a mist out of the coldness of ground-level confusion, that where it is least expected.

Goodness is found in the blending differences of routines, life at home, at the well, over the cook pot, yes, sometimes in war. Women do not go into war; does God? He must be about, whether or not He likes what goes on ... as often women are there or nearby. His people are there; foe and foe, both are of God, or are only Israeli humans of God, of His making? Are we speaking of mama, her place in the household; have we wandered a bit, or is this a portion of the life we share, male and female ?

You are aware a woman may not rule over a man away from home, especially at home – lest his image be damaged, if by chance one is maneuvered, the way for it to work is that he not admit to it, not acknowledge it.

Papa was in no such danger and made it clear. Yet, in some ways he allowed himself to be moved as a game piece ... you've not seen that in this tale? It doesn't happen in matters of love, that includes everything relating to papa's commitments. Anything relating to household matters he allows, except when he makes his periodic territory-marking-excursions within mama's fortress.

In families where female dominance happens and becomes known, the male wears the unbecoming label, a few like it that way, possibly not the label. Experience shows that men share serious thinking with women to harvest their wisdom without credit in public, it would not do, and women know it ... mama was left out of that behind the scenes opportunity.

With a few exceptions, woman influences governing only if man wears the trappings without her mark of making, considered right in the minds of men, accepted by women. In household matters, women with authority certainly are common. Even there, sometimes men dominate to the point of foolishness – a woman shared with me that her husband, *an intelligent, affluent one, insisted that she, also intelligent, eat every bite of her gruel portion or put it aside for later eating,* as though she were a child, or, worse, had no mind ... my God, how could she stand it?

How can the extent be known when the warrior's image must be so guarded? In all things he is first, yes, even at the hearth he feels compelled to countermand a decision from time to time to reassure himself. Intelligent women know this for what it is and retreat until the territory is marked and the marker satisfied, before they return to that which is theirs ... should be.

A whisper of female control crumbles the fabric like an old, dry skin, those clever enough to gain advantage usually are not so stupid as to waste their gain by flaunting – tempting as it might be. Qualification, we grant there are households with accepted feminine masters. (You think a female cannot be a master? You may have the point.)

Fabric crumbles for those stupid enough to cackle; cackling is reserved for the male in this story ... you thought it the other way? ... I'll admit, roosters crow, hens cackle and cluck – life is this way.

Mama did not cackle, she had no reason to, at first maybe she did, later she clucked, sometimes silently; eventually, I learned to cluck silently, though too late.

In early times, we didn't consider whether or not mama's household dominance was known outside our walls, inside she was in command – none questioned her voice, except, of course, when papa was there. When there, he allowed her control, rarely countermanding, in this he appeared secure, even with mama's calm command in his presence, usually ignoring him.

On her side, it may be that her knowledge of his prowess, or lack of, showed him human to her ... likely, few men are the great things they, or women, imagine them to be, including kings.

Someone must command at home; papa had other interests, as everyone knew. (Am I being cute? Not intentionally, however, he did have other interests, *and everyone knew*.) Had she been without skill in her territory, she could have chosen a servant who was, but that would have left her without purpose or activity. Some women go mad who find themselves in that unenviable existence, it is an existence without sympathy, to avoid it is simple wisdom, any drudgery is to be preferred.

Mama's position allowed papa freedom from household management, saved him worry about loyalty in that – loyalty being one of his greatest concerns; in fact, gradually it consumed him in spite of his diversions.

When did my education in the art of closet-command begin? Long ago, mama, of course, was my teacher. I can't tell you at what age I first began watching as she steered papa into hearth corners he would not have chosen, when the corner became too tight, often he lowered his horns and charged; then mama knew to run. The next thought shapes this one a bit more.

Always he appeared a trifle awed by her presence – usually masking it with sharp answers wrapped in resentment, occasionally rebuffing her, apparently to reassure himself and reestablish his emotional territory. Who knows how much that had to do with reducing his amorous interest in her? Does a man make love to one who awes him or one he resents? Was his concubine a means of separating love from responsibility?

Analyzing men's love potions is not one of my gifts. His concubine was nothing like mama.

Mama became extremely skillful except, of course, when it concerned papa's eye for women, in that she had no influence at all once the new wore off her own charms – which was happening before my time of awareness, yet sporadically she tried, long after I became aware.

It was a pleasant surprise to discover almost by chance, that papa responded to my childish wiles with simplicity as though a nose ring were there for my use. For a time, I judged it a weakness to be exploited, *misjudged it*. Don't misunderstand, he was not lecherous toward me, not at all. He was gentle and loving early on as though my innocent face were a true picture of my mind. His girl children may have received his only tenderness (about his other family in their privacy, I do not know). In childhood I knew to guard the image he created of us; it was precious as gold, worth more to us. Does that disenchant your image of childhood?

His illusion was partly true, but not all; our innocence blended with, fed incipient dreams of grandeur, he of all should have known that; but he visualized in his girls a continuing innocence he would not allow his women. Are all men so?

Merab was a lovely thing, wanting to be a mother from my first remembrance, so different than I, at first not realizing a male is involved, later liking it sometimes ... don't ask how I know that.

Does that embarrass you? If so, these tales will be too much for your sensitive soul, say so, we will quit now ... you are still here?

We both adored papa Saul, certainly, we knew he was male, he had the privileges. He was grand, petting, loving us, telling what fine queens we would be, using wiles to shape his interests. We believed his promises of great things ahead for us, he loved us in his fashion. Our husbands would be exactly like papa: big, handsome, kind, loving; yes, dull mama was forgotten, as we imagined a beautiful future through his promises.

Rolled sheep's hide became our children, oh, I joined in her make believe, I was a child, too, *a female child*. My question seeds sprouted early, but a child's mind molds its dreams of fairy prince and princess, pushing aside doubts that blur the dream. As they waited patiently at the door, sometimes I cracked the opening to wonder about them, question them, passing sustenance, sensing their reality – mixing the innocence papa painted with some awareness of what crouched in waiting ahead.

I wondered how Merab and I lived the same life and saw it so differently, we saw the same deceptions; saw mama hurt each time papa discovered a new package. Don't over-judge papa, he was a good man; mama caused some of his wandering with her resentment wrapped in sharp words.

Yes, eventually I learned from mama, Merab appeared not to, mama crooned the same sad song to her ear and mine. Merab meekly accepted male fickleness as inevitable, a burden females tolerate. You thought I didn't learn from mama?

Am I speaking of mama the drudge, the placid?

"Prepare yourselves, my daughters, your lives will not be the beautiful tale you imagine, not at all! You'll be pawns in the king's game, to him, women are for his use, some for his enjoyment."

"He enjoys us, mama."

"Yes, he enjoys you. I know he indulges you and shares his fantasies with you, too but, beware, my daughters, I know his mind, it is not what you think. He's a shrewd, selfish man, always planning future moves, you'll find that out sooner or later. You will be traded for his ends.

"Men will want you, he will hold you up as a lure before the buyer he chooses. You'll be a chip in the bargaining of kings. Of course, they will want you. Before they possess you, they are one-minded, sending emissaries to sell their short-lived promises, any price, anything to get their desires. Women are foolish to believe them, remember, I told you."

"Papa is kind to you, allows you to do what you want, mama. Your life is not so bad, you order the servants around, have fine linen for personal things, how could you have a better life?"

"I could have time and attention from your father, even time divided with another would be an improvement. Male company on occasion would be pleasant."

"He gives you time, mama."

"Yes, he gives me time as he gives his chief provisioner time – one is equal to the other. I would have him speak to me about something other than household staff or family problems."

"Papa cares for you, mama, it is expected men will share with others than wives."

"Who expects such as that? Have you already accepted that your husband will have women conveniently spaced around for companionship? You, Michal', have been put under your father's spell, he speaks with a sweet tongue when so minded. I know from experience, though it has not happened of late."

"Did you expect papa to abandon the practice of multiple women? Did he tell you he would do that?"

"Not exactly, but he left that impression; when he wanted me, I thought I was the only one he cared about."

"Do you mean you had a choice in the matter, you and he decided? Between you, you discussed the marriage pact?"

"Oh, no! You know the bride isn't asked or talked with of those things usually; but there are ways of knowing. You'll see."

"Often you talk with him about us, you're not being fair with him."

"It's no use explaining to you. Another wife would be more acceptable than this, we are abandoned for one without a name."

"She has a name, why do you say that?"

"But not the name of 'Saul', a nobody has moved ahead of us."

"Is it not better that he has no other wife? We could be sharing our position with other families in addition to the one with no name, would that be better?"

"Now you're being practical, once you include yourself in the problem, you join reality. Continue that, and you'll see what's ahead."

For long I believed papa, his endearing, "*My little queen,*" lifted me from hide dolls to a throne in a twinkling, papa loves me; he's the kindest most loving papa in all Israel. His tongue painted beautiful life, whirling, glowing rainbows became jumping ropes, then stretched taut for hanging girl fantasies, impossibly transforming them into milky moon-fluff pillows in golden tents, tiptoeing through his planted dreams among whispering breezes. He caressed us with words, high and away from problems – *when we were children* ... mama wasn't in those dreams; actually, neither was papa, the papa there was another fantasy.

Earlier, did you infer *no interest in babies* from my thoughts? That isn't quite so, with me it isn't an either or, although other things loom larger many times. My babies would be angels, becoming fairy queens in real fantasy kingdoms. I joined Merab's sheepskin imaginations with my own versions, different endings.

"Here, Michal', this is your baby," and it became a cooing infant in my arms. My skin-babies never cried.

In that regard, Merab was the more practical, "You smell litter as aloe," I said.

She denied it, "Every baby dirties and cries," she said.

I knew that. Everybody dirties and cries, everybody hurts and joys, everybody births and dies ... but not I, not my babies. Papa Saul and God are friends; God loves us, so we're different. Papa tells me of his plans to smash the Philistines, of the great things to follow for him and me; no one but the two of us as he spun dreams in my open imagination.

God has promised papa a great kingdom; he goes with papa, protects him.

"Yes, daughter, God often comes to me through Samuel." As he became involved in telling, his fists mimicked the strong gestures of Samuel relaying God's messages. "He instructs me in tactics I would never dream of using without his help, never on my own would I send home a portion of my troops. Yet, we defeat them, kill them, smash them." His fist strikes his palm.

I notice, too, his face is red, his eyes clouded, tension increasing him a span up and broad.

"Does He never speak to you directly?"

"Of course He does, but in a different way; usually when Samuel is not available."

"How does He speak? Do you tremble?"

"I'm not to tell that to anyone, not even you."

"Not to Samuel? When you tell Samuel what God said, does he believe you?"

He walked back and forth as he gestured, with that, he whirled to me, another span greater, "Are you doubting my word?"

"No, papa," I hastened. "I know you're truthful."

But I doubted, only the prophets heard directly from God, papa is not a prophet; he is papa, though he makes me shake sometimes.

Papa's wars are like my babies that never cry; his wars never hurt because God is with him. He smashes the Philistines as they deserve,

MICHAL'

God takes care of His chosen and hurts the others; *He is papa's God, our God.* Papa Saul told me so! Do I believe him?

Now you know: I wonder if papa always talked with God or sometimes only thought God was speaking when it was his own emotions.

He swelled with confidence when he told us of God's orders, *other times it was as if he and God did not know one another. Often his actions did not taste or smell of God – that when he roared loudest.*

"How can God be so close one time and not answer your call another? What is it that causes him to love you and then quit you?"

"Who are you to question that, have I lied to you?"

"I never accuse you of lying, papa, I question if you could be mistaken."

"One is as bad as the other in relation to God's guidance, a mistake could destroy Israel. I will not admit either."

When the God-appointed king says God is speaking, who am I to question? You likely are a better judge of that than I.

Strange that papa often talked to me as if I were an adult, he opened his dreams, even his battle plans to me, *stranger still since I am the questioner.*

Yes, I questioned him even then, almost did I say, '*except not about his speaking for God*', already I told you it tickled my thoughts that early, his varying confidence indicated that he, too, sometimes questioned if he were hearing correctly.

Eventually it became clear why he talked to me: he needed a sympathetic ear, one that could be cut off if it offended, my ears were in danger often. He was a blend of bravery and insecurity; soon that knowledge became a long-lasting peril to me.

Why did he choose me to hear his musings? Why would he open his words to me as though I were a sheepskin to be written on? Then, I didn't question, yes, I just said I did, usually in a deep mind-cave only, now to surface for chewing and softening, as the sheepskin he wrote on.

Why didn't papa talk to Merab? He did, of course, but more the way he talked to mama; words that dusted their minds, never laying down tracks or patterns from his depths, only I shared those – and likely Jonathan. Those tracks grew bushes with thorns as time went on, those, too, I shared; have you seen the thorns in the brambles already, felt their sting?

Remembering now, it's clear I was his closest friend at the time, probably the only one except Jonathan, though always he was surrounded except in home privacy – and, likely, second home privacy; I don't know; later that made it worse, harder to approach him.

Hopefully you've grown accustomed to these wanderings, we cannot abandon them, since they are the reason for our tale. How can a woman survive if she finds no outlet except through female functions? Am I too plain speaking, is there a better way of saying it?

That is my problem, God placed an active mind in a woman's body – in a world that has no place for such. We might be better without; though surely there are many. What happens to them, how many adapt better than I?

(That is an interesting thought – bodies that function without thought, not limited to one sex, certainly, *for, men, too, are destined to live in a world where thought is not prized except to promotes the ends of another,* a world where the body has more value than the soul ... and that in a nation that follows the one God?)

Did I say I am tall like papa? I accept my height, it goes well with my mind, I revel in both, I am blest in those; if only He had better suited me to my opportunities. God will not call me to be king.

When God smote his enemies for him, papa had difficulty believing himself worthy; doubting, fearing; distrusting that he deserved God's blessings – yet determined to keep the crown at any cost. If only he could have carried the confidence his victories earned, he wanted so much to be great, feared being forgotten in years ahead.

He never accepted himself as equal to his great presence, always doubt cast shadows on his successes – thereby twisting his mind, clouding decisions, causing fearful judgments and hurt.

MICHAL'

I watched him as he pounded his head with his fists. "Papa, stop! Are you trying to knock yourself senseless?"

"My head aches fiercely. It has happened more and more of late, God has put demons in my head to punish me."

"Why would he punish you? Have you disobeyed more lately than before?"

"There you have hit it, never have I been sure God spoke to me about being king. That's why I hid in the baggage, not because I was timid."

"Samuel would surely tell you if you were not God's choice for these times, papa, have you looked at your likeness in the pool? Do you see a small man in God's eyes?"

"I see myself, daughter, I tremble before God – his people I can deal with, chew them and spit them out if necessary."

But it was not so; he doubted himself as their king which increasingly showed in his dealings with them; standing before me, turning with storm winds of the mind, is the great man, now a child beside his own child, I pick up my sheepskin doll; at once I am his older sister, the only one who can encourage him, shaking, I release the doll, it falls to the ground askew, I realize he has put me in danger.

A child knew that? Somehow I knew, there was a storm wind, the hurricane of his emotions, shredding the tendrils into frayed strands, whipping them into shard fragments, hurling them, piercing those he loved. At the moment I was the nearest, most vulnerable, not again the innocent; of necessity defensive. Once more the sheepskin doll is hugged to my immature bosom, shielding a maturing heart.

"I have never known a braver man than you, papa, you are not afraid of God." With those words, his slumping shoulders slowly lifted as from weariness, his mighty back straightened as from sleep.

"You are right, child, even God does not frighten me, it is fortunate you can see it."

And so it was, fortunate for him, *more for me.* Soon I talked to my doll babies as papa talked to me, Merab scolded, cautioned me to think girl thoughts ... I tried, sometimes succeeding, my thoughts extended beyond changing diapers, even of ordering households of servants. I watched mama do those, she thrived on them, I would not.

Where does that leave me? In cold mountain pastures distressed by bitter winds, though then I didn't know.

Oh, I had my day in the household, ascending the ladder of command was normal maturing, learning the tricks of leadership came as naturally as breathing, first skin dolls, then concubine offspring – yes, including the boys from the other household.

How was that when they had a separate abode? Things shift about; you should know that from your own life. You know about harems, about wives and concubines. You and I aren't that different, even though I am Saul's seed, many of the differences you see are imaginary, over the years I've learned that.

How can I speak so assuredly about our similarities? You and I are one, the wrong whim of the right person crumbles any life including mine. Spilled milk on any fabric sours, hardens, and becomes brittle; you will see as we walk together.

How can two households with a parent in common be so near and not sooner or later acknowledge one another, even become friends? Only warring parents keep them apart; sometimes that will not. Rizpah and her growing family, moved into next abode from the king's residence. He could have moved them in with us; mama never gave him credit for that courtesy. For that matter, neither did I.

The king's wayward seeds by his concubine inevitably would become playmates for his children. Papa may have intended it so. Mama made it sound dirty at first; as a result we snubbed them, carrying out mama's torn emotions. How does one see cleanfaced little boys playing together day after day and think them dirty? They were little boys with big smiles when they saw us.

"Can you play with us?"

"May we, mama?"

"You have other things to do."

Someone forgot to tell them they were not like the good people whose children are married; the holy ritual of song and dance. They asked again, with the same open smile, so much like papa's when at his best.

We forgot to ask mama and played with them. We became friends, papa appeared not to mind, mama grimly looked the other way. Eventually, sometimes they joined us around papa when he was

MICHAL'

in a sharing mood, and mama, too, finally saw them as children, any children, even to including them in loose family activities. I suspected she grew to love them, at least cared with warmth, oddly, eventually they called her mama as we did, and she didn't correct them. The first time papa heard it, he glanced quickly at mama, probably expecting an angry reaction. By then it was common, and she responded as though it were normal; his eyes widened, but, wisely, he said nothing.

Their mother, Rizpah? She never intruded her presence, evidently secure in papa's company, wishing not to put it in jeopardy. Or, possibly, she had a sensitive spirit and wished not to hurt mama further.

It is difficult to see papa as that caring about mama's feelings, or am I mistaken? Often I have been, though, who knows? If the children could be accepted, why not the mother?

When Merab came under my sway is difficult to locate, it happened so gradually.

Another, 'not exactly so, either.' I remember very early making suggestions that guided our activities. On the other hand, never did she completely come under my sway, probably because my needs were so different from hers.

Both played with dolls but with different notions of what was taking place, to Merab they were babies to be loved and changed – the making of life, fulfillment of dreams. To me they were dreams, too, plans for great things, ways to share men's being and visions, to make them mine – their visions.

Mostly, I didn't chase men in my fantasies; sometimes I did, however. *"No one is a whole color melon; I least of all."* You may know that already.

Later, I became a whole color in that regard as I dreamed of David. (That is our one difference, yours and mine: I never entirely thought of him as King David. Always to me partly he was the boy who first came to us, simple, unassuming – *though I knew better; yes, I knew better as time went on.*)

Jonathan shared with us in his early years even though papa frowned on girl activities for the future king. I liked it when

Jonathan got us into games of war, Merab was listless in it, letting me carry his armor and weapons, to my delight.

"You carry his weapons, Michal'. You're larger than I, anyway."

"They aren't heavy; why would that make a difference?"

"I thought you'd like to carry them; if you don't, say so; give them to me."

"I'll carry them; don't be churlish."

"Help her, Michal', she isn't made for armor bearing."

"And I am? I'm teasing, give them to me."

Was he more like me or Merab? At times one and then the other – always to my surprise. That applied to both of them. Am I confused? Let me explain ... no, if you watch carefully, it may explain itself as we proceed.

If only I could see your mind as you hear this, is doubt there? Some sharing? Envy? Likely even the male mind would find room for understanding, if not sharing. *There must be some wonder of innocence in men*; though little is seen in their dealings with woman. I have known the dreams of two kings, my father and my husband. Also, I have enjoyed the attentions of the one only to lose him, but that is ahead of our story.

(I strive to be discreet so as not to offend your sensitivity; but if we are to have a story, you must learn to accept accounts of personal life, prudishness may be a virtue, nevertheless it stifles communication.)

There is more to the tale than these childish memories, after the telling, you may agree there are boulders for stumbling, undreamed of without the telling. We continue....

Papa spent much time with his children telling and re-telling of his rise from a common searcher of lost asses, to be king of all Israel, *ignoring that he was the son of a rich man accompanied by a servant while searching for the asses.* Poor papa, only one servant with him on the search, he was so poor (or forgetful) the servant provided the shekel for a courtesy gift to Samuel when they approached him.

"*Here I have with me the fourth part of a shekel of silver, and I will give it to the man of God, to tell us our way,*" he said to papa. You know, he wasn't yet our papa at that time.

Now, at the time of telling to us, he was well aware of the impact of that chance encounter, its potential in legends.

Did God drive off the asses in order to bring about the fateful event? Papa hinted of that possibility, laying the seed for great fields of speculation concerning Divine ordering of important events, who is to say it is not so?

Yes, he shared much of his remembering with all of us – counting those from the other side of the mat, in that, he acknowledged the need for legends if a dynasty is to begin. Likely, they were as proud of their papa as we, though not favored in the inheritance line.

No, no! I knew no woman would sit on the throne of Israel. He included females to ensure wider retelling of his tales, he already had plans for us in mind, from mama's warnings we suspected, but refused to believe.

Women as well as men, or better than, can repeat tales to children who will tell other children, including their own later, fanning out into great numbers. Such tales brighten dull evenings about a hearth-fire, extending to distant campfires, warming cold nights and lonely hearts.

Indeed, what do women talk about at the well each day? Legends become so by repetitions, not by burying under a rock marked by a desert bush. Those are soon buried in shifting sands by winds of fresh events. Lively legends tossed into up-draft winds soar as a falcon, stir imagination, eventually make their own wind, stir a self-fueling flame.

He liked to stand when telling his anointing story, assuming a pose as though speaking to his generals, he told of how God had spoken to Samuel about a man who would become first king of Israel, of his (Samuel's) conversation with papa, of his own humility when told of God's plans for him to be that king.

Oh yes, papa was modest, astounded, but likely trembling with joy muted by disbelief and doubt of himself. Papa was from one of the humblest tribes of all Israel? It was the smallest, otherwise pure modesty ritual, certainly not humble after papa became king.

"Can you see me there, Samuel beside me spinning the beautiful web of events marked by God?" he asked.

"Oh, yes, papa."

He told of being found and brought in, of sitting as chief guest at the feast, of the anointing by Samuel. Clinched it with a tale of God's touching him with the spirit of prophecy, the part of which he was most proud – his prophesying experience in which he was drunk with the Spirit, you know of that, of course.

There was that huge man naked, as he tells God's words to his hearers, how that must have improved his image with them! Beautiful body or not, I question that God wants it in raw display publicly, though, a few lascivious women may have rejoiced

Much later he repeated the holy performance, lying many hours without clothes to hide his nakedness to all who passed by.... *Please, may I question that God told him to strip naked and lie in a stupor equivalent to drunkenness as a sign of anointing?*

I do not question that God was there, their response is my point of question. Did God want that, or did he take what came rather than alienation? What choices do immature minds give him? And who is to say they were not drunk on spirits of the grape as well as the spirit of God? Maudlin behavior has more than once accompanied delving the wine vat, treading the vat prepares in quantity, sipping in quantity leads to drunkenness, maudlin drunkenness.

Drunken prophecy may be thought by the prophet to be of God ... *does God say it so?*

Papa tells the story for truth; *true or not, it influenced the rest of his life,* time and again he overstepped his bounds as king into the realm of priestly functions, every time it brought trouble! Am I belittling God's privilege and opportunity to enter the lives of His people? I deny that absolutely, it is misinterpretation or misuse of God's work for personal ends that disturbs me. Papa was not above that ... it was clear as his inner picture was revealed through crazing line-patterns of time.

At my perspective over two kingdoms, both claiming God's guidance even sometimes into soiled ends, *the question remains.* Holy lyrics and otherwise notable lives do not change the question raised about drunken prophecy, the doubts about God's full wishes being carried out.

When the means and ends are not according to God's

Commandments, where is his presence? Remember that question as this continues, also remember that this tale is tinted with hues rubbed from characters of great passions.

"When I returned from the search for lost asses, I kept my peace about the news Samuel told me about God's plans, in my modesty I found it difficult to go through all that with these who had not heard God's words through Samuel," said future King Saul.

Pompous papa! I could guess why he kept silent: he knew no one would believe him.

"Samuel talked around the bush before telling me what God had planned for me, as though he were concerned that it might frighten me away. I was not frightened of course, but very humble in the presence of God.

"And astonished beyond measure, look at me," as he spread his arms above our heads in his blessing stance. *"Do I look like a king?* In the beginning I could not believe God had such plans for me, who was I but a simple man of the humble Benjamin tribe?"

No one in Israel looked more like a king, and he knew it! If all else were equal, though, one of less stature could not have brought the quarrelsome tribes together.

What a story it was; how Samuel later went through a long process of selecting from among the twelve tribes, finally to that of Benjamin and among all the men of that tribe before identifying humble simple Saul – actually a giant among fellow Israelites.

Reviewing now, it appears to have been arranged to sell the appointment to Israel, else why since he was already chosen by God? It succeeded – not necessarily to our benefit in the end, though, who would reject such a sweet lightning strike? Certainly not Saul.

Lo, he was not to be found when the call came. Oh yes ... he's hiding among the baggage. How reluctant he was to become king ... and who would begin this legend if not papa? Who else would know the details? Papa was not stupid about promoting his fame, that shy man was not papa – unless fear caught him.

This sounds like ridicule? Not at all, would I ridicule one I loved? Besides, I knew papa well. Should I say only what people expect to hear? Plain speaking applies not to intimate topics only. He was not always brave, if you think that, you've believed carefully polished legends without hearing unflattering nuances. Or possibly the version you heard withheld them. See if this is not so.

Oh, I know, papa hearing these thoughts, and in the end David also, would have been my death. Solomon, too, would step on me for my wandering words – but I am beyond such fears, now I face only one – no, two: myself and one other, oh, oh, am I so old, to know Solomon?

I said love was not involved in my story? Again, not entirely true, I loved papa Saul very much, though that love has changed over the years. As he became two persons, the love could only be with one of them – the other was not loveable.

That, too, must be modified, *always he was more than one*, else why would he begin so early to set up his girls for trading stock in his game of kings? Why would he use us as tools for spreading his legends? Why would he have two families, or more ... why?

Where was the solid core, the heart of Saul that God saw? Always he (papa) saw individuals, including those closest to him, as tools for moving his ideas, for promoting his ends. Is it possible for a person to be so consumed with his own ends? *It is possible.*

Even Jonathan felt the impact of his swings from sincerity to intrigue although he was less the receiver of intrigue than Merab or I. Being the first male he was never trading stock, none of the males were, of course – that honor is reserved for the other branch of humanity.

Now I wonder why God chose papa and allowed long leadership when his greatest attributes were wrapped within his commanding presence, when He could have terminated it at any time.

Papa was handsome; have no doubt his bearing was that of a king! Yet, Samuel had experience already in hand, with no spells of madness; *he was fallibly human, but not mad.* Placing the mantle of God's anointing on him would have been simple unless God disqualified him for temporizing about his sons' sins as judges.

Even so, I was glad it was as it was, for without King Saul I would not have been a thimble-size influence in the kingdom. Better to have lived with small glory than be lost in a faceless harem. I try not to think of that possibility too much, it frightens me; not the loneliness or loss of male company, more the becoming one among women without faces or minds, probably so for any in a harem, *I would go mad.*

I am aware of the impact I made on Israel's story, even though my influence was interrupted and limited.

It may seem strange to you that Jonathan was not jealous of the attention Papa gave me, for one thing, it was not his nature, for another, he understood that I could never be his rival for the throne.

Women live and work at a different level of life. They dance for men, marry, if they are fortunate bear children, and run a household if the husband is wealthy. If he is not, they are servants or field hands as well and intermingle their housework with gestating and raising the brood of children.

Their bodies and minds are so made, the difference is marginal except in the ease and comforts available to one or the other – constrictions of the mind are the same. I say again, "I would go mad in a harem."

Before we leave this thought: I'm aware that I mentioned only the mentionables. There are other women who for one reason or another become objects for men's pleasurable use. But those, of course, are beings without feelings, minds, souls ... if they are not in the beginning, they become so. Why did God let them be born, you ask? Are the men who use them better off?

How much does God have to do with their lives? Their becoming? Are their lives what he intended? *Whose life is what he intended? Why do so many of us alienate God when it is obvious his blessings are lost when that happens?*

Jonathan understood that I was no threat to him, as did I; though understanding did not make me like it. He accepted me, I accepted him, neither of us was responsible for life as it is; neither would change it greatly. Surely, he understood – Jonathan was not feebleminded, even if at times it seemed so.

No, I am not casting envy at Jonathan, it is that later when his future as heir to the throne was in question, he appeared not to care, I find that difficult to grasp.

Papa was not like Jonathan, he found Jonathan's lack of ambition as confusing as I. It was particularly difficult to understand when Jonathan was so great in war, papa was too. Should not great generals be great kings? Papa was a great general and could have been a great king; did God get what he intended when he called papa?

Always papa's ambition waxed strong, though his confidence alternated with insecurity, no, I haven't forgotten the *'hiding in the baggage'* incident. I've already explained that.

It was exciting to share his developing plans. Jonathan, too, shared these plans for war – not plans for his own reign, unselfish Jonathan loved war. When papa talked of when Jonathan would be king, he listened; papa probably thought he was being properly respectful of his elders.

"I will take two thousand with me at Michmash, a thousand will be with Jonathan in Gibeah, the others I will send home, with God we do not need them."

"They are so many, papa, our men are so poorly armed. How can even God prevail against such power?"

"The Philistines will not overcome God, little queen."

"How, papa, what will he do? There are so many of them."

"I don't know yet, he will make it known when it is time. Did he not find me among all Israel? He will go ahead of me."

"You have great faith, papa, I don't have that kind of faith; God has not shown himself to me."

"Of course not, I am the chosen, the Israelites will joy they have a king when they see how God goes before me … you will never have faith, Michal'."

He was not right, in that it was Jonathan who won the first great victory after papa became king; for papa it was his own.

Already, his fame came when he cut up a yoke of oxen and sent parts throughout the land, bound securely with threats to do the same for any who did not join against the Ammonites. Brilliant, merciless strategy, instantly establishing his leadership, foreshadowing a trait soon to become widely feared: *his ruthless blood lust.*

Quickly that won the army he needed, and his first victory. Visions of their own oxen dismembered made instant soldiers of hitherto reluctant farmers and herdsmen. A live farmer with dead oxen plows little ground; better to risk war believing he will not be one to die, the soldiers magically materialized from hiding, establishing Saul as commander and great leader.

Would papa have carried out the threat? Apparently they thought so, I agree – *stories circulated that he put out one eye of captives taken in war.* That bloody example got the army needed but did nothing to convince them of God's presence. The people of Israel did not share papa's faith in God's attention.

When reluctant recruits learned of the properly armed Philistine multitudes ready to crush the poorly armed motley army of Israel, they ran for cover, any cover – they hid in wells, in caves, holes in rocks, even in tombs among the dead. It is amazing how a nation of men can vanish so quickly, so quickly forgetting their fear of dismemberment.

Indeed, papa himself lost confidence; it was then a crack appeared in his shield, what I saw as evidence of uncertainty, others may have considered decisiveness. He panicked and assumed the priestly role when he saw his army running for cover – performing holy ritual in Samuel's stead. *Remember, I told you so as you see him repeating hasty action.*

Samuel immediately perceived papa's arrogance and called the great one to task as though he were a child. "*What have you done?*"

Another flaw appeared, "*When I saw that the people were scattering from me, and that you did not come in the days appointed … I forced myself and offered the burnt offering.*"

That did it. "*Now your kingdom shall not continue,*" said Samuel.

When papa recounted the story he skirted that, except in moments with me. It didn't come out precisely that way, but it was so.

You might expect God to leave him immediately. He did not, instead God allowed it to go on for considerable time, many years in fact. During those continued years, his mental stability deteriorated to the point of consummate madness.

One wonders why God delayed after speaking so through Samuel.

These years later, it is possible to speculate at a different meaning of the "*shall not continue*" edict, apparently, he had the dynasty in mind rather than Saul's personal reign. Looking back, that appears the only explanation.

The other options: that God might have been joking, or only threatening? *Not to be considered.* God is not a simple parent over and over threatening flogging to disobedient children.

One other possibility: that Samuel may have been speaking his own emotions into God's message, twisting God's words. He, too, was human, though we little like to think of God's spokespersons as fallible, we want to think the tube-straw from God to us is flawless – only in ourselves is flaw allowed. (You doubt Samuel's weaknesses? How quickly we forget the reasons for Israel's cry for a king.)

It is so easy to misunderstand statements, possibly even those relayed from God. Those relaying the message may inject their feelings or poor memory when speaking, in that case it was, should I say, *may have been* Samuel doing what papa so often did.

Evidently the alternative – speaking personally to everyone at once – is not the choice of God. If he would but do that....

How did I get into that? I am a poor judge of God's plans or methods, had God consulted me, he would have laughed, possibly he would have thought better of it and made me mindless, as I likely deserve, sometimes am.

In one of the continuous skirmishes with the Philistines, Jonathan secretly went out on a mission with his armor bearer. Between the two, they slew twenty enemy soldiers, causing great panic among them.

Jonathan told me about that. From that hammer stroke of resoluteness, I was sure Jonathan was ready for the next step: becoming king after papa. Already he showed marks of greatness.

Papa joined the battle and claimed full credit for the victory. Jonathan gave no objection, he never appeared to be jealous – of papa, me, or David. What a king he would have been!

Naturally, as papa's fame grew, he became more sought after by women. You expected it to be the other way around? It was both ways, the reality is, fame has its double effect, adoration attaches a special aura that would make a homely man attractive, and papa certainly was not homely.

Neither was he built for singleness of affection, he realized his physical lure to women, easily could have been much more promiscuous. Others now revered as Godly examples have been worse in that regard; strangely, that is overlooked as being expected in men, even those venerated as closest to and speaking for God.

Singleness of amorous attention is eulogized but rare in a society that accepts multiple wives and concubines, papa did no more than one might expect under the circumstances.

Am I defending him after expressing doubts about his character and ability?

Certainly, he was my papa, I have a right to be upset with him, to discuss his weaknesses. Also, I will defend him.

Are morality and singleness of affection the same? Is God involved in multiple women for men? Does he approve, or allow? If he allows, is it the same thing in the end? What does it say about God's opinion of his other half of creation? He did make both sexes, did he not?

Is the permission for multiple women truly from God, or is it man's wish of what God would allow? Was it a man or woman who heard that message from God? (I can make a good guess on the last one.)

You say it sounds as though I have no faith in anything or anyone. Does that preclude normal reactions? Must those most affected be as oxen driven before the plow? Most of my life has been used up walking that furrow at the gee and haw of another.

May I puzzle about life, the life in which I am involved? I've always done that, but I didn't do it orally until too late to matter.

Must I be consistent? I am consistently inconsistent, I am a realist; also, what I say is true – of the facts around me. My opinions, of course, aren't to be confused with facts, sorting them shouldn't be too difficult, alike as we are, you should do that easily.

All this rambling may be making me appear a poor mate prospect, let's see how that holds up in the end.

Merab and I were together more than with Jonathan, because papa often included him in king's activities even as a child since he was heir to the throne. What better way to prepare him?

It was clear papa trusted him, because he was given command of troops very early, little more than a boy. Always he trusted him – *almost always*.

In spite of that, Jonathan and I developed a relationship that served well when papa's wild swings of personality surfaced; exploded is closer to fact. (Brothers Abinidab and Malchishua were with us but not singled out for special attention. Ishvi was different yet.)

Do I repeat myself? Sometimes a trace memory says so, but you will understand that; if not now, later.

Our mutual trust may be surprising, considering my bent of mind. In truth, it was comfortable and necessary, we both needed a confidant, few were available. To each other, we found it easy to expose threads of what others would call treachery, without fear of misunderstanding.

Such openness allowed mind patterns to be spread on the raw surface of conversation for peeling and examining. Wiping away was instant and sure, in that, never could I fault Jonathan. With others, that would have brought disaster, they would have reported treachery in what was nothing of the kind, only we understood each other so well. (Oh, yes, his loyalty to me wavered; but what could he do?)

One big difference in us, Jonathan's relationship with papa lasted to the end. (Had our bodies been reversed, much would have been different; but they were not. In the end, I believe we both were content; possibly God, too.) Mine was intermittent – and worse, papa's myopic trust betrayal interrupted our understanding. Unfortunately, my poor judgement played a part in our disintegrating friendship. The outcome was extreme, I would not have believed my life could change so much.

How did papa betray me? If you know the story, that is evident without explanation, if it is not yet clear, hold on, it will be eventually.

Jonathan would have been a good king, at least he had loyalty, courage, and trust in God's leadership, *who else would have gone only with his armor bearer to challenge the mighty Philistines?*

When he told me about that sortie, it was with his usual serious but casual mien. "It came as an inspiration. Had I paused to question, I would not have had courage for such a thoughtless act, usually I am neither afraid nor foolish, when I said, 'Come, let us go over to the Philistine garrison on the other side,' my armor bearer responded without question, in that moment as thoughtless as I."

"Did God speak to you?"

"Papa laid it to that, I make no such claim, more likely it was a foolish impulse."

"You don't have foolish impulses, brother."

"Everyone has foolish impulses, even kings. Don't make too much of me, you'll give me a swelled head, we need no more of those." I could tell he was serious. I marveled at his wisdom and bearing.

Hardly could the Philistines credit their eyes when the two alone approached their troops.

"Look, Hebrews are coming out of their holes where they have hid themselves."

With that, they made a great mistake by inviting these two lonely Hebrews among them. Those two slaughtered twenty, the others fled, beginning a panic which engulfed the garrison.

Papa saw the panic, wondered who had caused it, counted, found who was missing from his camp and with gusto joined the butchery of Philistines. With this, excesses of human slaughter became everyday practice among these followers who claimed to model God.

Is my searching for God's hand showing too clearly? Are you not a seeker? *I am not doubting God,* it is papa, whom I know so well, who brings about these questions. That he claimed God's hand is not in doubt, that God ordered the slaughter, is my question. Again, look at his Commandments; are papa's deeds consistent with them?

I forget that Jonathan, too, was involved in slaughter, though he never claimed God's involvement in any way. It is so easy to attribute to God those things we do from desire. It is so much wanted to believe our leaders are in touch with God. If they are not, where are we going in these excesses? If not, God is frowning on our intemperances – how discouraging.

In this instance I do not remember papa saying God commanded it, that came afterward, when he had learned the excitement of killing. (David, too, soon learned the lure of blood. It was seen as early as when he appeared before papa holding Goliath's head by the hair – by then, dripping-blood drying in hanging strings.)

This time it was that the Hebrews who had defected to the Philistines, returned to their own kind and those who had hidden in crag and crevice came out – I'm speaking of the others who returned from their fear, when papa and Jonathan now established themselves with glory in war.

Is it any wonder papa Saul treasured son Jonathan? How I envy him the glory of the campaigns. The killing, too? It was necessary, it is the claim that God ordered and blessed it that disturbs me. It disturbs me that in holy war, *herem*, God orders slaughter to the last living thing, it does not appear consistent with his wisdom, is it possible his spokesperson, his followers did not understand?

Would it not be easy for God to set a wall between peoples, or to push the enemy away with a blast of wind? Or simply to roar and frighten them away? I do not understand.... But I am not God, neither am I his appointed prophet or king, I am only a woman who has come to sadness, aching, seeking, sadness.

Killing has finally reached me, involved me, too late do I seek God – oh, how I hope it is not too late! Now I see David's turn of mind, his ambivalence, hunger for God; but this is later.

Yes, Jonathan would have made a good king had he not been cut short, musing on this also saddens me; I must turn from it.

Now again, papa Saul made a mistake. In the midst of a campaign, in the midst of killing, without telling Jonathan, he charged his followers not to eat again until it was evening and full vengeance had been heaped on the Philistines. In his usual plunging haste of decision he said, "Cursed be the man who eats food until it is evening and I am avenged on my enemies."

You know what that means, slaughter! Would you rather not know? If we avoid knowing, possibly it didn't happen? Come now, accept reality, when has God given man license for revenge? Papa is moving ahead of God.

How could Jonathan keep an oath he did not hear? He could not, did not, yet was held accountable by papa as though Jonathan had broken a promise to God.

Would God be unreasonable with Jonathan about something he had not heard? If he did, then I am the one who does not understand and to be held accountable. My questions run ceaselessly when told about God's thinking – *as reported by papa with his own interests. I doubt papa's unbiased reporting on anything that could have a remote influence on his plans, or in defense of his actions. (If God did all that papa said he did, I am undone by my questions.)*

Too often has papa lied or changed his stories – papa, not God. Have I gone too far again? I could say he misled us, would that satisfy concern about parental respect, and about God's part in his actions?

Back to Jonathan: In his resentment, brother Jonathan disagreed with and criticized papa Saul. He should not have done that before the soldiers, even though he did what he thought was right, for the soldiers grew faint from hunger and therefor sinned.

"My father has troubled the land; see how my eyes have become bright, because I tasted a little of this honey. How much better if the people had eaten freely today of the spoil of their enemies which they found; for now the slaughter among the Philistines has not been great." (Always it is slaughter. Jonathan was not averse to that.)

In their hunger, the soldiers ate meat without draining the blood. "And the people were very faint; the people flew upon the spoil, and took sheep and oxen and calves, and slew them on the ground; and the people ate them with the blood."

God was angry with them for their sin and would not answer Saul. This is not something Jonathan or I can argue with God about, I argue with papa, with his already wandering thinking. In this case I was not there and could not remonstrate with him.

Surely it was eating without draining the fresh meat that caused God's anger, Jonathan knew about that rule yet allowed it because of their great hunger, *it was wrong.*

In this part, papa displayed rare perception by showing no favoritism even though his own son be the one who must die for leading in sin. But if Jonathan did not know, was he guilty?

How would papa know who was guilty? Already Jonathan was preferred among the soldiers over papa; not a soldier would tell, not one! Yet, by using Urim and Thumim, it became clear he was the guilty one.

"*Tell me what you have done,*" commanded papa of Jonathan.

"*I tasted a little honey with the tip of the staff that was in my hand; here I am, I will die.*"

With his decision papa showed his fitness for kingship, he said, "*God do so to me and more also; you shall surely die, Jonathan.*"

Many times I have said papa would not kill his sons, I'll never know if he intended to carry out the promise. If papa was serious in his decision to kill Jonathan, either his agony was complete or his parent mind was gone – a real possibility.

Much later I faced a similar loss and almost went mad of grief. You will hear of that in time.

Of course the people would not allow it, papa appeared not too hesitant to accept the will of the people in this, another disobedience, his quick acceptance of their plea for Jonathan's life throws doubt on papa's sincerity. Surely no points were made with God by accepting the plea to let him live, over God's command – unless the killing is not always God's wish. There again, you have a basis for my doubts.

At this very moment the thought arises, did papa plan this strategy as a means of cementing the affections of his followers? It would not be beyond him, even to quoting things never said by God, if so, it was another early sign of madness, who in his right mind would misquote God? Yes, who would misquote God?

You don't believe it? Follow our story; tell me what you pick up about his sanity and truthfulness along the way, even of intruding on God's preserves, read it, read it everywhere.

Am I doubting God's part in this? Not at all, only papa's reporting. There is no doubt that God was with the Israelites and, with papa, led them when hope was low. There is less certainty that papa always reported accurately.

Papa became great as a warring king, because of that our people, continually endangered by the Philistines, followed him, still he confided in me, his second girl. Why?

Without this, I would have shriveled to a husk, already my interests had passed the limits of household gossip and turmoil – *why* would I betray him as he later claimed? He was my encourager, my hope of a future!

Fortunately, I realized that household intrigue and the tumults of war are of the same family. *While my men warred*, I daydreamed, hoped for threads of change in my life; while they warred, I lived as women live.

Have I told the 'why'? No, only more of my turbulent thinking.

My men? Yes, my life began climbing the narrow stairway of *complication*, a stairway without handrails, with step treads as fragile as crisp autumn leaves. Each tread appeared anchored, yet ready to float free with the slightest breeze, to drift in autumn winds ... at this recalling moment I tremble....

Is my life as fragile as those stairs? How sure is my step? When will a tread release from its moorings and float free as a thistle seed, where will I end? I'm thrashing trailing strands of eternity with whirling questions, fearing answers are beyond finding. If so, that will cast me free into unending space of the mind in all directions; only answers will draw me again to calm with God where peace may find my heart. In searching eternity, my mind feels the immensity of space as questions float away, grasping for a hold on God. Because I am a woman, will God not hear me? If a woman *could* talk to God ... if God *would* talk to a woman.

"If you would be great, papa, our neighbors on every side should feel your strength."

"I draw men to me, my men soon discovered cause for fear; already my name causes trembling among the Philistines, God directs me and punishes those who oppose me on the way. His instructions to '*not spare them, but kill both man and woman, infant and suckling, ox and sheep, camel and ass*' will make me great in the eyes of men. Yes, Michal', you shall be a queen."

"*Even infants*, papa?"

"Every one!"

"Are you sure you heard right? Even animals?"

"It was clear."

"Where will I be queen, papa?"

"I will show mercy to the Kenites because they gave kindness to people of Israel when they came out of slavery in Egypt."

"Did you hear my question, papa?"

"I have not decided."

"Will God tell you if you ask?"

"He allows some decisions to me, leave that to me, child."

With that, he turned to duties of state, isolating himself from family responsibilities, next in turn he went to second-family interests; I saw him enter their house; yes, I was watching, as was mama. That evening he did not return to us or mama, by then she may not have missed him, or did she?

When papa made the decision to be lenient with the Kenites, he again made the mistake of disobeying God's instructions by *not destroying everything* among the Amalekites.

Possibly my questions about God's instructions caused him to hesitate. No; that is unlikely in that it was not infants spared – as I had questioned. Instead those things spared were of the covetous nature, including the best of sheep, oxen and the fattest of the lambs. Otherwise he utterly destroyed all the people with the edge of the sword.

(Does this bother you, as it does me – now? *It is factual reporting of what happened.*)

God may have been searching for obedience in papa; he may have forgiven papa for a show of mercy to babes, *but not covetousness, unless papa mis-told God's instructions* ... but he wouldn't.

I sympathized with papa's wish to retain some of the spoils of victory, it would not be easy to destroy food when your soldiers are famished, even if God's goal were known. A hungry, complaining army seems closer than God sometimes, and supplies are difficult to come by. Besides, God chose papa, doesn't he owe papa some leeway?

Papa was birthing unruly traits of arrogance as God gave him victories – I saw this and recognized trouble ahead. Yet, had I been on the field with them, my vision would have been as theirs – clouded by hunger. A growling stomach is not easy to ignore when food is at hand, yes, I understand, – *but did God?*

Papa's magnificent presence increased with each victory. Mama's pride in him waxed great, then wilted as his eye turned to another fig. And, again, she turned to household activities, doing her best to accept life, failing that, doing her best to dull her mind – or was she dull at birth, dulled to survive? Women see papa, he could not resist, he had no reason to try – women presented themselves to him – multiple females, harems, were the custom, taking was as easy as picking a fig or an olive and then another, and spitting the seed, he was being a normal male.

Females were doing what they could for any gain of position, though temporary; *in hope of advancement – one of the few ways possible.*

Mama lifted her head again, turned stolid eyes to survival; she was queen of the king's household if not his affections.

Camp prostitutes plied their trade without hindrance, though not approved by God. I asked papa about them. (How did I get here? isn't it obvious?)

"What is a camp prostitute, Papa?"

I could see the twinkle in his eye. "Do you not know? You are no child."

"Do you see them, Papa?"

"What?"

"You know; do you see them?"

The twinkle disappeared, "Of course I see them, they are close behind our troops as we travel, I move about all parts of the company."

"That isn't what I mean."

"Are you prying into my private life, daughter?"

"Am I not your little queen today?"

"Michal', you are treading on dangerous ground, such things are not discussed with one's family." The easy was gone from his bearing.

"Who are they discussed with, papa?"

"Certainly not with one's children, especially not a daughter."

"Did you just say, I am 'no child?'"

"Does that make my private life open to prying?"

"Papa, I'm not prying, I'm asking about life; are prostitutes not people, our own people? Have you closed your heart to them, as to me?"

"They are people, everyone goes to them, that is why they are here, would we have an army if men were deprived of that pleasure? Would men face death otherwise?"

"That is a cost of war? Do the prostitutes return to normal activities when there is no war?"

"When will there be such a time?"

"Is that the lure used to recruit armies? The men leave family and safety for danger because other women become more available to them?"

"Certainly not."

"I thought you said that is why '*men face death.*'"

"I did not say that; you bend my words. How could they return to normal activities when it is known how they have occupied themselves."

"Then they are consigned to perpetual service, to the needs or wishes of men, they are a price of war, a special price."

"They are not forced into servitude, no one has captured them, they wear no chains."

"Why are they there, papa? Where do they come from?"

"They are paid for their services, they are those who have no other future, those who have forfeited normal lives, they are fortunate they were not stoned earlier."

"Yes, papa ... and the ones who use them, what is their price? Where do they come from? Were they, too, fortunate not to have been stoned?"

"They are not selling themselves, they are my men – husbands, fathers, and brothers of everyone."

"No, papa, they are not selling themselves, they are buying. They are our husbands, fathers, and brothers ... do they return to normal activities between these episodes of invading foreign soil and women? What of the women overrun by these lusty conquerors? Are they treated with respect? Are they allowed to decline the honor?"

"I have seldom used either, I have little need."

"You have lost such desire?"

"No, I have not lost such desire; I have friends and admirers, as you must know."

"That is much better, do we have other brothers and sisters?"

"That is not your affair."

"My brothers and sisters are not my affair?"

"I have allowed you more freedom than you should have, that is clear. You are prying into private matters; we will discuss this no more."

"I'm sorry to have pried, papa. Our brothers and sisters are not my affair, if they are not acknowledged."

He left our discussion with less than a twinkle in his eye.

Would you agree my place in papa's confidence has allowed unusual conversations between us?

In that discussion I was treading a thin line, at a later time, his mood may have been more explosive under such questioning, fortunately, he was calm now.

Who but I could question him in that fashion? Probably not even Jonathan.

Papa knew my person, may have guessed, yet did not know my dreams. If he did, he ignored them, because he knew they were wasted, wasted by his plans already firmly set.

Why wasted dreams? Women have no place in genealogies or wars; oh yes, occasionally mentioned, *his wife was so-and-so; she produced children.*

You protest that men are listed because they fathered children? True enough; why are not names of mothers listed, the son of mother and father? Is mothering less significant? To me it appears at least equal, why are not daughters listed?

Listener, don't tighten your stomach, don't be upset, my dreams are not that great. I can live with the limitations, though I chafe a bit under them (need I say that?). One way or another, we expand our boundaries, my boundaries changed several times, sometimes expanding ... again shrinking.

Had papa realized the depth of my questioning, he would have chosen another for private conversation. On the other hand, it was my bent that brought our minds together. Why did he choose a girl? Over and over do I question that.

CHAPTER III
BEHOLD, I HAVE SEEN A SON OF JESSE

David was a beautiful young man. How did we get to that from the last thought? Rather than tell you in a cold rush of words, let's go back to the excitement that led to my first view of David. It's quite a story, you may know some of it, though not from my words, some of it you have heard already.

It was like this: After papa became king, his anxiety caused an evil spirit to torment him. A manservant with a gift of discernment diagnosed his problem and suggested the lyre as soothing ointment for his torment.

Another who had heard David play described him so: "*Behold, I have seen a son of Jesse the Bethlehemite, who is skillful in playing, a man of valor, a man of war, prudent in speech, and a man of good presence; and the Lord is with him.*"

As quickly as that, it was begun. We see from the servant's report, *David was not solely the shepherd as he claimed when explaining why papa had not heard him sing before, or, as we like to imagine in our "shepherd-boy" fantasies.*

David came to Saul, joined our household, as you heard earlier. The instant I saw David my heart leaped, for here was a youth of beauty whose touch of strings also touched the heart, whose magic rippled in all directions, captivating everyone with the spell of youthful innocence, nearly everyone. (I saw him long before he saw me, besides I was yet a child, but not in my own eyes and not for long.)

As you heard, his play on the lyre soothed Saul's violent spirit, causing him to love David, quickly to make him his armor bearer and musician.

Thus began a long but stormy relationship between papa Saul and David.

HIS PRESENCE WAS GREAT

Our brother Jonathan also loved David at once. Almost every member of the household was affected in time. The moment he entered our family, relationships had a different lubricant. At times it brought stormy competition; other times it was calming oil on the waters; sometimes they blended, gradually cooling, once again to separate into non-blendable parts – for they were as animal fat in hot and then cold water, unable to blend permanently, though in the same bowl.

That was David, to see David was to feel peace and strength, to know David was to become involved in excitement, few ever again to live in peace – some, many, not to live at all.

I wanted David the moment I saw him. This was to cause me unending problems, beginning almost immediately. It would have been more peaceful to be a wife or even a concubine in a rich man's harem, papa Saul chose that I not be – he saw other uses for me.

As you know, papa had plans for David that left me out. What of my lead-ring in papa's nose? Somehow he discovered and removed it before it was any great use to me, or he was playing mind games with me, possibly much less under my sway than I thought.

David, being the youngest of the sons, went back and forth from serving King Saul, to his father's pastures near Bethlehem to tend sheep. Likely, while there, he provided court gossip for his papa Jesse's pastime, fortunate and envied were those with such news sources. His mama? She likely heard and assumed her role of news-bearer at the well, the normal role, increasing her among the women.

I need not say that while David was away, another carried papa's armor, when he returned to Saul, another tended the sheep. Why David's father did not release him from shepherding duties is difficult to understand, in view of the honor papa Saul granted him. Possibly family jealousies entered into that, or, as likely, Jesse enjoyed his news source at the court. Women are no more prone to that than are men, though men would make us believe otherwise.

In any case, that is how David first came to us. Who would have dreamed this beautiful harpist and singer would change our lives so? Who would have dreamed he would frighten papa as no other? Yes, in the long run, even more than did Goliath, papa shuns that topic as though it never happened.

Our time was made for men like papa and David, the heathen Philistines with their idol worship and constant attacks, either overestimated their own abilities or overlooked that God was on Israel's side. Also, they gained courage from their victories, which kept them returning.

Time after time, their hoards swept upon our people, until fear seized us, we clamored for a king to save us from our enemies – papa was among those calling for a leader, little suspecting his role.

Then came the message from Samuel about papa Saul's future as king. Our lives flip-flopped, papa moved into leadership, for which he was not prepared except by his great presence, and he was ripped and torn by his unready emotions as he ripped and tore his people and his enemies.

David came, our lives churned and whirled, the household never again long at peace … but now we're talking about papa.

Papa often overcame the Philistines in battle but never could conquer them, God would give him victory in one place, only to find them arrayed against his armies at another with the job to do over, and killing continued … and continued.

It happened again at Soco of Judah with the armies facing each other. The Philistines camped on a hill, and Saul with his soldiers of Israel camped in the valley of Elah. It may be, the Philistines were growing weary of defeat at the hands of papa's armies. When Saul won, he made sure they remembered. It was war, to lose was to suffer, to die. We won and lost, many of ours died.

In a stroke of genius, the Philistines sent out a champion named Goliath of Gath, a giant clothed in armor from head to foot. His javelin of bronze with a shaft like a weaver's beam was slung between his shoulders.

"*His shield bearer went before him,*" Goliath took his stand and with great roars challenged the armies of Israel to send a man to fight him to the death. Whichever was killed, his people would be servants of the other.

(A comment here, lest it be forgotten, is there record of the terms of agreement being kept by the loser? Nothing changed in that regard; other changes were vast, again, other changes....)

"I laugh in your face, warriors-like-women. Send your greatest one to fight me to the death, choose him with care, for he will return minus a head; I will carry that to my king, drag it in the dirt from whence it was born, where it has lived, and dogs will chew off the ears and nose, worry the meat, eat it, gnaw the bone. If you have one with courage, send *him* with trembling knees. Send him that I may eat him.

"The gods have blessed me as the mightiest of men. Send your greatest that your maidens may laugh and ridicule you; that they may beg to polish my armor, your women will ask to wash my tunic and comb my beard, you will serve the Philistines tonight."

At this, papa Saul lost courage, was dismayed and afraid, and his men. *Would you expect this to remain a secret in Israel?* This went on for forty days, each day the threats more lurid. None stepped forth to accept the challenge, *not even papa Saul or Jonathan, is it any* wonder desperate measures would be considered?

Without knowing his role, David's father, Jesse, entered the battle from Bethlehem. He sent David to carry provisions and see to the welfare of his three older brothers who stood trembling before Goliath in the army of Israel. David went to his brothers, after one of the interludes when he returned from papa to tend sheep for Jesse, while he talked with his brothers, the giant again roared his challenge. David heard it.

You know the story; everyone does. It will be told and retold as long as men live; *it is a true legend. Certainly, women will tell it, too,* of course you've heard it; yet it must be told here because it shapes all that follows. (At this moment a woman tells the story, not the first time.)

Forty days of roaring challenge, forty days of consternation, of fear and trembling. Even brother Jonathan? Yes, even Jonathan, even great King Saul! *Everyone; like a devouring beast, fear swallowed the mighty men of Israel,* they were frozen as in stone.

Honor forbade treacherous attack on the challenger. A dozen, nay, two dozen soldiers may have overcome him, but consider the cowardice it would reveal. On the other hand, consider the cowardice already revealed, fear confused their minds, reduced them below treachery; a weak, aged one could have done better.

(Remember one half of Israel was not considered – the lowest boy servant would have come first. Would one of those not considered have accepted the challenge? You wonder, could I see myself there? Did I not say I am a woman at heart? *If you question that, consider my womanly response to the one who seized the opportunity now.* This is useless musing, not a complaint.)

Continuously they puzzled about what to do ... who would oppose him? Not one stepped forth from Saul's great men. "...*Have you seen this man who has come up? Surely he has come up to defy Israel; and the man who kills him, the king will enrich with great riches and will give him his daughter, and make his father's house free in Israel.*"

What a reward! What a lucky man that will be! (Here is the place for women – a reward, value; a plump hen to be viewed, this thought was farthest from my mind at that time.)

Notice, they did not say which daughter. *I knew it would not be I.* That was already decided.

David questioned, "*What shall be done for the man who kills this Philistine and takes away the reproach from Israel? For who is this uncircumcised Philistine, that he should defy the armies of the living God?*"

His elder brother heard and accused him, "*...I know your presumption, and the evil of your heart; for you have come down to see the battle.*"

Had he, too, forgotten that David spent much time soothing the king's torment? That he no longer was *only* little brother?

"*What have I done now?*" was David's reply. Only time revealed that he was not as innocent as he appeared, nor should he have been after time among king's companions as lyrist and armor bearer for papa.

He must have had amazing confidence in himself or equal trust in God's hand, anyway, David's blistering comments about the pitiful situation of the trembling Israelites were repeated to papa, who immediately called David to him.

David offered, *"Let no man's heart fail because of him; your servant will go and fight with this Philistine."*

At this point, I wonder what Papa would have done had he seen the future with the anxiety David's success caused him, *he should have known any man who could defeat the giant would become an instant hero, overshadowing all who stood trembling, including the king and his son heir.* Thrice as perilous would be an innocent singing shepherd boy turned conqueror of the giant.

Fear paralyzed them, including their reasoning, they thought even a sure defeat of their greatest or least, at the hand of the giant would be better than this groveling before Goliath. Surely, courage in defeat is better than cowardice.

Did papa intend to keep the terms of agreement if defeated?

The boasting boy who claimed God's hand upon him stood no chance against the mighty mailed warrior; yet, let him try, what is to lose except a youth – and their freedom? What choice did they have, after forty days of trembling?

David's claim of God's assistance may have swung the balance.

Why not call on Samuel for guidance? Yes, fear paralyzed their reasoning. Was Samuel awaiting an invitation to assist, or was he also paralyzed, including his advice? So many questions without answers.

What a sight it must have been as they piled Saul's armor on the youth, who never before had worn such. Off they came, *"I cannot go with these; for I am not used to them."* There he stood, youthfully slender, outwardly confident, wonderfully proportioned, not papa's size, but certainly not small. What went on in his mind? Had God truly spoken? Evidence favors that.

You know what followed: then he took his staff, selected five stones for his sling and went to the Philistine giant. Oh, had I been there, but to hear it told, now to remember stirs my blood ... my David calmly standing before the giant without fear.

I said, "my David?" That was a slip of the tongue, *he was not my David.* Every maid in Israel yearned for this comely boy-man, *most called him "my David."* Papa knew I loved him, *and I knew that if the impossible happened and David were to overcome the giant, papa would give Merab to him.*

The impossible happened. As David stood before him, Goliath shook with anger that he should be insulted so, *a mere boy coming before him, without armor. Only a woman coming to challenge him could be worse. (They, the overlooked, trembling for this brave, beautiful boy sent out as a sacrifice.)*

He cursed David, his fury clouded his mind. David's cool words surely sounded as child's prattle to Goliath, instead of waiting for David to come to him, he went to David.

"Your head will be roasted for my feast this night, served by a new Israelite slave. The tongue will be appetizer; the hair will garnish the whole of it. A sparrow would provide more food than you. Look and tremble, your last look, you are cut down, your blood will sour the soil."

Surely David's eyes sparkled at that, a stone already nestled in the sling ... that was it! The sling whirled, a stone flew, Goliath fell, it was over – except for hacking off the head, done with the giant's own sword, long feared, now a memento symbol of portents affecting two kingdoms. The beheading took longer than the battle and was more gruesome, severing a large neck is not easy, even for David.

That may have been the first human head David removed; it would not be the last. Where had the practice come? Beheading bears, he said, a not uncommon activity, but early indication that 'beheading' held no problem for him.

In that moment, a timeless legend was born. Our lives were changed forever.

What was the brother thinking who said, *"I know your presumption ... you have come down to see the battle."?* Each brother, every soldier, once it was done surely knew he could have done the same, but did not, and forever was envious of David.

Confusion reigned among the troops and spread to the entire nation, confusion and joy; joy and worship; worship of a boy become man, a man become hero. What becomes of a boy who overshadows mighty Saul?

According to terms of giant Goliath's challenge, the loser's

MICHAL'

people were to become servants of the victors. Would papa have taken his people into captivity had the shepherd boy been killed? Of course not, neither did the Philistines become slaves of our people, the war went on and on.

The purpose rendered was quite different; was it God's plan served up with the help of Goliath to introduce this hillside shepherd into history? If so, Goliath the loser paid the price, gruesomely sacrificed for David's infant career.

In war, there are winners and losers, as in life, the path chosen (or born to) determines the options. What does that mean? David's brothers could have volunteered, and did not, had one done so and succeeded, how different would history and my life have been? His brothers, too, were beautiful but swallowed in fear, as the others who stood unprepared, trembling, wallowing, whirling in uncertainty. Did I know them? Not then.

I wonder how long it took papa to realize what had happened. Was that realization the beginning of his mental imbalance? I believe it was, for papa asked Abner, commander of the army, *"Abner, whose son is this youth?"* as though he had never seen David before. Great gaps appeared in his memory and reasoning from that day. Abner apparently joined him in forgetfulness when he, too, denied knowing this one who had been among them as the shepherd-musician, entertainer, poet of distinction. *Either that or he thought it politic to go along with Saul's confusion.*

David replied as though the question were normal, *"I am the son of your servant Jesse the Bethlehemite."*

It was then Jonathan formed an alliance with David that never wavered, even when David was under attack from papa. Not even when papa questioned Jonathan's loyalty, though that never appeared to sink deeply into papa's love for Jonathan ... their friendship lasted to Jonathan's end.

Possibly intending to destroy David by giving him responsibilities he could not fill, until now untrained slingshot warrior, papa immediately elevated David to command troops, opening opportunities for triumphs, quickly seized. Everyone applauded, including papa's servants. *Yes, and his children* ... no, not papa.

What do you imagine Saul thought when a new song was sung among the people?

"Saul has slain his thousands, And David his ten thousands."

What would you have thought if you were king? *Exactly!* Papa was angry; soon he went out of his mind, raving even while David played his lyre as before, no longer quieting the distraught mind, now a burr under the blanket, even as a lion growling in his tent. How can I under-speak so carelessly? He was a pack of burrs imbedded in a festering new sore in papa's own hide, a sore that never healed. The nervous lion crouched, never slept.

Twice while David played his lyre, papa tried to pin him to the wall with his spear.

Twice David evaded him.

Guards moved between them as with little boys, though it was far beyond that with a sharp spear in the mighty hand of Saul, lunging at David.

David hastily sped out of there, was David frightened? I would have been. No man, not even David, could have remained calm under that constant barrage of uncertainty: papa repeated vows of appreciation for David's ministrations, suddenly interrupted by violence, attempted murder in the presence of the court retinue.

Somewhat papa came to his senses, though his suspicions of David remained. With David's popularity among the people, it was difficult to remove him completely.

And David returned to resume playing and singing as though nothing had happened, but something had happened: barely concealed was explosive tension.

So, papa appointed him commander of a thousand to get him out of his presence, an insignificant command intended to relegate him to obscurity. From papa's point of view, it was a mistake, David succeeded at everything; soon he was more greatly loved. Daring successes combined with a boyish air of simplicity, though no longer a sling-shot warrior – how quickly his fame spread, wafted over the land as a refreshing breeze in the morning. Again an understatement – it was as a hurricane whipping papa's emotions as it inflamed wild acclamation among common people hungry for more of this simple boy-man, lyrist, killer of giant Goliath.

As they say, papa had grasped a bear by the tail without intent and couldn't let go.

What to do? Bold measures exploded from papa's desperation; schemes from his mind and those of his jealous generals filled and cluttered their thinking.

The planned outcome? Drug his caution with reward and acclaim, put him before the Philistines in battle; let them dispose of him – notorious tools in politics and illicit love.

Abner reminded papa, "You promised your daughter to the man who would slay the giant."

"What would that accomplish in the dilemma we're in?"

"Merab would be a potent drug, the sweetest wine you could offer, his reflexes would be slowed, your spear point would not miss next time."

"You're right, Abner, but your thinking is limited, we'll use her better than that."

And papa said, *"Here is my elder daughter Merab; I will give her to you for a wife; only be valiant for me and fight the Lord's battles."* (A tool often used in politics; daughters, I mean.)

My heart cried in anguish; I had dreamed of a miracle that would put me in Merab's place, yet, here was Merab's delicate beauty, masking nectar, offered to nascent innocent urges ... *nascent and innocent as ascribed by hero-hungry Israel.*

Only later did I learn of the scheme to put David's life in danger, papa was not alone of our kings to try that; David's memory proved good years after, when his own desire was for a woman who belonged to another.

My heart sank like a stone. David had seen Merab and her delicate beauty; there was no chance he would not accept his prize.

"You are in great fortune, Merab, every maid in the land will envy you, even I."

"To be given to David for his wife? What does it matter, one or another, it is not men I love, but babies. Another will do as well."

"You are not normal, Merab. He's the pick of the land, any woman would rejoice in your good fortune."

"You may have him, I'll tell papa."

She told papa, at first he did not believe her; his answers were like mine.

"You're out of your head, daughter, any woman in the land would trade places with you. The man has accepted you, you must go to him, or I'll have no face before my people."

"Will it be worse than sending a boy to fight the giant in your place, papa?" His face purpled, mouth opened, no word came out. I was there, watching, afraid for her, disbelieving, both what she said, and his response, expecting he would pin her with his sword if he did not fall first with a stroke.

His anger did not subside, he gave her to Adriel the Meholathite for a wife.

As I said, we did not know where that was ... we learned soon enough.

You would expect David to be angry at papa's faithlessness, perfidy. If so, he hid it well as he went about the warring-killing business assigned him, any anger he had was taken out on enemies assigned by the king ... have you forgotten what he was doing to fill his time, to vent frustration?

At first I could not believe my good fortune; surely an angel had prepared Merab to open my way, otherwise, how could it be? Earlier I marked some of our differences, mentally and physically, I knew we were different, yet nothing prepared me for this.

"Really, Merab; why have you done this? No one can care so little about the man she marries, have you chosen another? Will you do better? Have you no interest in men at all?"

I learned more about her in the next little while than in all our time before. More would come later, much later.

"Michal', have you considered that we are handed out as a piece of cloth? No one asked me if I wanted David, neither papa nor David."

"Would that have made a difference?"

"I don't know, it's too late to find out now."

"Will Adriel suit you better, can you reject him if he doesn't please you?"

"I don't know, I've not seen him ... no, papa would have me put to death if that were to happen again, I hope I like Adriel."

"Did you not like David?"

MICHAL'

"I don't know; it didn't become an issue."

"Was that not the issue?"

"Have you heard a word I said? All our lives, you've lectured me about having no mind of my own, now that I do, you don't understand."

"This is not the Merab I know, have you become a different person?"

"You ask that when I do the only thing possible to be noticed when my life is being decided? Is it so great a thing to say, 'This is my life you give away.'?"

"But Merab, you have rejected the most desirable man in the kingdom."

"Have you considered, *rejecting a shepherd or field hand would make no statement at all*? Rejecting David will never be forgotten ... where are your magnificent ideals when it counts? Are your thoughts so cheaply sold? *Take him, Michal', he is yours."*

So quickly we forget, '*rejecting a shepherd...*' she said.

All my ideas about Merab have been chopped into bits and scattered in strange corners.

Anyone would know her decision changed everything for her, and everything for me. My way is now open; never would I have dreamed of such a choice, which way shall I go?

Should I follow Merab's lead with an equal statement, declaring the humanity of women? Nothing in history would equal what we could do to change men's view of women, two daughters of the king rejecting the most eligible man alive – *unheard of.* What an impact we could make!

In a twinkling, my lofty thoughts were sacrificed; as quickly as the desires of a serving maid, *my mind was full woman.*

There was a problem: papa didn't think of me as a woman, though larger than Merab, I am his baby girl; yes, larger than Merab, physically mature, still a child to papa. It is one of the puzzles of life, fathers build fantasies about their daughters, illogical, stupid, but there they are.

Again Abner spoke with papa or it would never have come about, "Have you considered Michal' as suitable for David?"

"Michal'? She is a child."

"Have you looked at her lately?"

"You are right, he may like her as well, why have I not seen it?"

"Everyone else has, including David."

Papa trusted me, or he would never have put me into a position of such influence with David, of course neither he nor I knew what would follow.

Once again, servants were sent to inquire of David's interest in becoming son-in-law of king Saul. Had he or papa inquired of my consent? *Of course not*, no more than they asked Merab.

David's response once more was favorable but guarded, implying no great eagerness:

"Does it seem to you a little thing to become the king's son-in-law, seeing that I am a poor man and of no repute?"

Such modesty from the one of whom songs are sung over the nation, of his killing ten thousands, slayer of Goliath, legend maker! *"...of no repute?"*

Hindsight shows David to be far-sighted, determined to do anything necessary to gain his ends. At the time, however, that was not apparent, papa acted with no knowledge of what David had in mind, of his real interest in the alliance, it is barely possible David didn't yet know, either.

Papa put the price of the marriage present (Is it price?) from David very low to insure it would not deter acceptance. That is known as *'leaving money on the blanket'*.

"Thus shall you say to David, 'the king desires no marriage present except a hundred foreskins of the Philistines, that he may be avenged of the king's enemies.'"

"Very low," I said? One hundred Philistines who would lose their foreskins may have considered it very high indeed, since they would not give them up without first giving their lives. Being heathen, they prized that which Israelis lopped and discarded. If David went on the mission, which he did, then papa's goal might have been accomplished on the killing, lopping mission, but it was not.

Once more, are your sensitivities offended at my words? The record shows it happened exactly as I said. How would you have it told? Have you accepted yet that we are telling a story as it happened, not as it has been reported romantically?

MICHAL'

Have you accepted that history is bent to the favor of romantics? That way it is sweeter in the telling and hearing; and not incidentally; that way it suits the ends of powers that be – men with their reputations and offices to maintain, fortunes to build, dominance to guard.

History bends to serve romantics and powers that be? This offends you? Are not empires at stake? Of course, romantics suit their own dreams, it may always be so.

By now, killing or maiming a hundred Philistines was as routine for David as for papa. It was all in a day's work, or a few moments – with his thousand and growing. Were God's orders involved in this simple venture into enemy fields?

Papa had not expected it to be easy at all for David, it was his hope constantly, each time David went to battle, that his problem with David would be solved by a lance of the enemy. It was not to be, this time at least.

Although the negotiations had proceeded normally, I could not believe it would come true until David appeared, not with one hundred, *but two hundred foreskins.*

Then I knew he wanted me; I danced with joy – in private, of course, for I watched from hiding. The cost of two hundred lives was forgotten, a goat or a Philistine, one as unimportant as the other when my wants are involved ... David is as good as mine. Am I confused about the number?

The only matter of importance was the hand holding out the bulging sack containing the full price, doubled. It was a messengers hand, not David's, he stood back to watch the effect, innocent appearing.

I have wondered how they were disposed of. Once received by papa, the purpose was served; they were no longer of value. My guess is, they were fed to the dogs; one raw meal for them; two hundred lives, heathen, of little value to David except for the cut flesh ... Oh, possibly they were cooked, a simple task in a pot, even out under a campfire.

Could it be that David paid twice the price asked as another way of demonstrating his ability, as a political move, not as proof of his love for me? Was he using me, as papa thought he was using David, and two hundred lives, or, was he a simple, boasting boy?

Not likely even then, though that is the inference often attributed to this flamboyant move. At the time, the thought did not come to mind that he might be making a well calculated early move in his game of kings. Time and experience broadened my thinking patterns.

CHAPTER IV
THE FIRST WIFE OF DAVID –
the lyrist shepherd of hillside pastures.

Thus began my part in the long-continuing contest between Saul and David, would I have been so eager had I known what lay ahead?

Papa had expected his troubles to diminish when his daughter became David's wife. It didn't happen that way, neither did papa's wish come true that an enemy lance would cut short David's fame along with his life.

David continued to win battles daily; with each victory his fame increased.

"...when Saul saw and knew that the Lord was with David, and that all Israel loved him, Saul was still more afraid of David. So Saul was David's enemy continually."

Nothing could dim my joy at being the wife of beautiful, wonderful David. We would have children, we would share the function of creating. A few times I wondered how much my love was influenced by the adulation heaped on him, quickly it was a passing thought, swept into a crevice of the mind by the convenient broom kept handy for such unneeded intrusions of conscience. I knew my love for David came from the core of my heart.

His golden tongue quieted my momentarily rippled feelings, "In you, my wife, my love, I've gained the sweetest, most beautiful rose in mankind's garden. God has blessed my eyes and heart beyond measure, never will I need another, never will I look at another, you fill my every desire, my everlasting love."

"Oh, David! I dreamed of being yours from the moment you came into papa's chambers. Yes, I saw you, though you didn't see me."

"And I almost missed you when Saul offered Merab. I could not refuse her, had no reason to since I did not know about you, that you were marriageable."

"You may have liked her better."

"No woman in the world would be sweeter, more beautiful than you, my love. To have missed this would have ruined my life, I would have returned to Jesse's sheep tending."

Almost did I believe him, I did, because I wanted to. He didn't know about me, second daughter of Saul? Of course he knew about me; how could he not? I will allow he may not have known I was available, wanting him, but, he knew, my looks told him as much.

I am wife of beautiful David, killer of Goliath, leader of armies. Every woman in Israel envies me – instead of Merab, *and except Merab*. We shared as man and wife, I waited expectantly, we shared ... I continued to wait. David and I both were sad that no issue resulted. Our love grew, as did our sadness.

Israel's armies moved about as needs arose, followed by the usual array. David's fame continually grew as battle followed battle, victory on victory.

Women saw David and admired him, placed themselves in his way. He had no eye for them, I attest to that, for I watched closely, even through the eyes of others.

We knew papa was not rational, that fears ruled him more than not. Now, David's music did not always soothe his spirit, may even have tormented him further.

After Saul's spear attacks, David never relaxed in papa's presence. Eventually we became aware danger was present when he was not with papa – the arm of a king is everywhere.

Everywhere there is someone who will perform a deed of murder for a price or hope of promotion, even against one as popular as David. Reluctance to kill is a trait harbored by few Israelis; those who might are reluctant to reveal the weakness, I'm speaking of men; women may or may not share the enthusiasm.

Being son-in-law of the king didn't bring relief as both papa and David had hoped – each from different plans, different dreams. Papa's fears grew in step with David's victories, as linked together as harnessed animals pulling a cart.

Fortunately, papa didn't cut me out of his trust entirely. He became more guarded, but I wasn't included in his fears.

"You are aware, my daughter, that your first loyalty is to your father."

"What of our belief that a woman leaves her father and mother and cleaves to her husband?"

"That does not apply when the father is king, your duty is doubled in that case. I count on you to see that my kingdom is not weakened."

"Do you no longer think in terms of strengthening your kingdom? Does this mean you are slowing your plans? We've had much pleasure reviewing your strategies for attack."

"That is a normal tactic of kings. This is not a usual time, with enemies on all sides; every rising youth may be a threat, even one's own sons." As he spoke, a twitch appeared on one side of his face; he felt it, his hand covered it as he turned away.

"Even Jonathan?"

"Not Jonathan, he's different; there is no threat in him, in fact, I've wondered if he may be reluctant to face becoming king when it's his turn."

"There would be no better king than Jonathan."

Jonathan continued to love David. Though David was popular, Jonathan was son and heir of the king – and known for his courage, except against Goliath. As I did not come by papa's girth, Jonathan did not come by his fears. It would have been easy for him to fear David; he did not. Jonathan's constancy in loyalty was remarkable. He carried the qualities of a king, God could so easily have placed him on the throne.

Why did He not? I would tell you, except God has not told me. For many years, papa acted less like a king than almost anyone in the kingdom, yet the heir to the throne wasted time carrying out orders for wanton warfare – often attributed to God. It is not my affair, but that does not stop me from wondering. We are a nation of followers, though questioning every step of the way; attesting to that is our history as questioners as we wandered during forty years of waiting to enter the promised land.

Papa both loved and feared David. Once his fear erupted into violence, there were only temporary respites from its random lightning thrusts; had I been David, I would have fled to another land. That David did not says either he knew he was to become king, or he didn't know where to run. Time would change that.

For periods of time, while papa was lucid, the violence toward David would subside. Then, again, it would explode, sometimes in cunning maneuvers to destroy David. As much as possible, David and I put papa out of our time together – it was not easy. David was determined but also human; even in the midst of our intimacy, he would suddenly comment on papa's wild actions, such interference made intimacy difficult, caused me to lose interest, certainly. *I would guess, he had already shifted away from the moment ... how could he?*

"David, why do you let papa intrude our private lives; is there no way to put him out of your mind?"

"It isn't a matter of 'letting him intrude,' he's already there. Removing him would require killing him, *that I'll not do.*"

"I didn't ask you to kill him, only to think of me when you're with me."

And there you have it, David's own code of respect for the king. Two hundred Philistines for me, tens of thousands killed while Saul's assigned under-commander of a thousand, but Saul he would not harm. There is a killing worm gnawing the mind of my David; I will soak the worm in love potions of my own making, drown it in honey, slow the killing urge.

Repeatedly the Philistines came forth to challenge the Israelites; repeatedly David led the armies in successes against them. Each victory brought him more acclaim, more confidence – and gave more distress to papa as David became inured to killing.

"How proud of you I am, David. But papa is not proud, he is more worried each time you return victorious. You might do better not to go out so often, or not to pursue the Philistines so determinedly. You know what you are doing to papa, a little less would bring you more."

"Are you telling me to lose a few battles so Saul will have less to worry about?"

"Would you do that if I were to suggest it?"

"Never in a thousand years!"

"I know; you aren't made to lose battles, have you ever lost in anything?"

"When I was small, my brothers played tricks that hurt – *yes, I lost, bitterly. Then I resolved to work at strength and skills until that could never happen again.* As they saw my increase, they ceased the tricks. They did me a favor by causing me to become strong; from them, my thoughts turned to wider pastures and larger flocks."

"Did your brothers accept you as a warrior?"

"They saw me as '*little David*' until I killed Goliath, as yet, not one has volunteered for my army."

"You could call them."

"I will not, we'll see how long it takes them."

"You say you long have known your pastures would be great?"

"With increased skill and strength came greater courage. It became a part of my pattern to weave, though I had tested it mainly on wild animals until Goliath, but not all; several forays with soldiers convinced me I was not wrong. Before Goliath, only a few had heard of me for more than music of the lyre.... Enough of this. I would return to sweeter thoughts."

Early-on, papa might have removed him, yet he did not. The distressed confusion in papa's head increased as David's support grew, chaos in his head already confused his great abilities. The decisive one who sent cut up oxen parts throughout Israel to gain his army became stew in the pot simmering on his own emotional fire – while David daily shoved straw under the fire with each foray.

Saul finally put forth an order to Jonathan and all the servants to kill David. He had waited too long, Jonathan could not do that to his friend. Instead Jonathan came to me twisting in agony; his face splotched greenish-white, moist with perspiration.

Together we devised an elaborate plan to foil papa's plot. I will relate our conversation as remembered.

"I am deeply alarmed, Saul's fears have made him a wild man. It is beyond mad thrusts of his lance; he's given out word to kill David. Even though the king's order, it is beyond my ability, help me,

Michal', what can I do?"

"If papa would rule his heart, his mind would clear, he is confused by his jealousies; if he turns on us, we're done."

"This call to kill David puts us in the desert with no water skin, Saul will accuse me of treachery because I'll not turn on my covenant companion."

"Brother, don't forget, he's my husband! David's restraint is amazing – with his popularity he might topple papa, both of them guess that. It makes papa wild that he doesn't know David's intent. I could tell him David does not entertain such thoughts; to him, that would be unthinkable treatment of the king ... *would that he could be as loyal to me.*"

"Is he not?"

"*He has been*, still I worry, he could have any woman he wants."

"The same has papa in trouble; he worries night and day."

"I'll not let myself do that, but how can I not worry when we have no issue?"

"You are right in that; it's a problem. A wife without male issue suffers a sad fate among our people, you're fortunate he hasn't put you aside."

"I see no way out if God doesn't answer my prayer; but papa's wild side is more pressing, *David must be warned!*"

"How can I do that? Saul has spies everywhere; every word I say is repeated to him, except these with you in private."

"I know! You must find a way to inform him without being caught up – *or I must. It would be better if you did.*"

"Even among the servants supporting David, always there is one who will report to gain favor, they don't perceive it puts them in mortal danger, more than the king's order. Saul's moods are unpredictable."

"I'll code a conversation with papa for you about his betrayal plans, for David to overhear. At last he may organize his supporters to resistance that will end his willingness to suffer persecution – I wouldn't blame him; papa has gone too far. But can you trust David with that information, he could become a stumbling block between you and the throne of Israel?"

"He is my covenant brother; no other is that. What must be, will be, God is in control."

"He is? Are papa's moods included?"

"I'm not so sure about those, nothing seems to control them, especially not papa."

"There is the problem; Israel shares it. *Could it be that God does also?"*

The results of our planning were so involved that I will report to you *in Jonathan's own words, first with David:*

"And (I) ... told David, 'Saul my father seeks to kill you; therefore take heed to yourself in the morning, stay in a secret place and hide yourself: and I will go out and stand beside my father in the field where you are, and I will speak to my father about you; and if I learn anything, I will tell you."

Then he spoke to papa Saul as only he could; he spoke well of David in these words,

"Let not the king sin against his servant David; because he has not sinned against you, and because his deeds have been of good service to you; for he took his life in his hand and he slew the Philistine, and the Lord wrought a great victory for all Israel. You saw it, and rejoiced; why then will you sin against innocent blood by killing David without cause?"

Papa trusted Jonathan and made another of his great mood swings, he swore,

"As the Lord lives, he shall not be put to death."

Again papa and David were reconciled.

You would think David would grow weary of papa's violent outbursts in emotions and lack of constancy, if so, he put it out of his mind.

Once more, David was with me and went out from me to war against the Philistines – those peoples who never wearied of attacking the Israelites – those who should be our slaves because of the bargain made when David killed Goliath.

Again David slaughtered and they fled before him. It was not in him to hold back even though he would have fared better with the king with fewer and smaller victories, he returned safe though those around him died. God watched over David, if not those around him.

As always when in papa's favor, when not away at war, David played his harp for the king's ease. It was as though he were still a shepherd boy with his lyre. It was inappropriate, incongruous – one moment, a commander of men; the next, a servant minstrel of the king. Or, is that the way of all leaders, a servant, a boy still to someone?

In that thought, the eyes of some reveal their confusion when they encounter me, even a few yet today who know who I am ... was. That, too, is incongruous; no one in the kingdom is less dangerous than I now.

Our beautiful love flourished; David's attentions to me consumed my thoughts when not with him, the time together was not enough. I dreamed of a little David at my knee. Would offerings at the altar bring fulfillment to that dream?

It happened again – evil spirits gnawed at papa's mind as David played his lyre.

Again he took up his spear and lunged to pin David to the wall. It does not require a great mind to know papa was unbalanced, who would do such in the midst of soothing music? Papa did.

Behind David's calm exterior was sharp caution, for the attempt was no more successful than before. His quick move evaded the thrust, no one's reflexes are better than David's. Once again he fled to me, how I welcomed that, reading much into it.

I remained within the trust circle, getting information about plans to kill David, as though I were not his wife. Knowing my thoughts as you do, you will not be surprised at my action.

I told David what was being planned, knowing he would go from me again.

"If you do not save your life tonight, tomorrow you will be killed."

Papa was not as trusting as I thought, suspicious finally.

Anticipating our move, he posted guards at the gate, making passage through there impossible, whether because of guards' loyalty to David or through carelessness, windows were unguarded.

It was easy to assist him out a window on his way to escape, as a precaution I put a goat's hide image in his bed. My interests would have been better served not to have done that; for without that I may have remained free of papa's anger, I, the bright one, acting in panic because my David is in danger. How emotions muddle the mind.

To make it worse, when the messengers came to take David, I told them, '*He is sick.*' I should have known that would not water the donkey. The messengers returned from papa with instructions, *"Bring him up to me in the bed, that I may kill him."*

Then I knew the hide was torn, I had no choice but to take them to the room, where they found my treachery. I stood trembling before them, they, common soldiers; I, the hapless daughter of Saul trembled before them.

Soldiers, arm of the king, authority; daughter of the king, fear weakened knees – one on each side grasping an arm to prevent flight; more appropriately, to hold me up. You expected me to march along with head high, to lash out at papa for his treatment of David? I would flee if I could.

But where would I flee? I'm not David, I'm a woman never away from papa's dominance, never free of it even when with David. Finally, do you see me now like yourself? The flood engulfs me, being dragged to King Saul in his rage. *King Saul – not papa? Not papa! I saw nothing of my papa in the violent man before me.*

He asked with quieting anger and sorrow, *"Why have you deceived me thus, and let my enemy go, so that he has escaped?"*

"I trusted you more than any other, Michal', and you turned on me."

Trembling, I replied, *"He (David) said to me, 'Let me go, why should I kill you?'"*

He did, he said that to me as we planned how to save ourselves. Now my David was gone, and papa no longer trusted me.

For a time, I thought he would kill me in exchange for David; as you see, he did not. The alternative was not greatly better, though I continued to remain in the household while he considered plans for my disposal ... at least I remained where reports of my husband's activities were discussed, not always to my pleasure.

I refused to think about what might happen to me, instead, I worried about David. Reports came back that David had joined the prophet Samuel again in Ramah, where it is said he took part in prophesying. Was he being political, or was he honing his relationships with God? Why must they always display their nakedness, are they truly doing the will of God when that goes on? Possibly David did not join in that.

Saul remained determined to destroy David, sent messengers to take him, when they arrived for David, they saw Samuel and others of his kind prophesying, *"...the Spirit of God came upon the messengers of Saul, and they also prophesied."* They also joined in the display common to prophesying, lay naked in the streets.

Quickly they found themselves in deep trouble with papa, *three times Saul sent messengers, three times they prophesied and forgot their task.* Their temporary loss of memory became permanent when they realized what they had done, where they would end, they had no place to go except to wait for Saul, and God.

These events could not have soothed papa's frustration fueled anger, though I was no longer in his band of trust, it was not difficult to know of his fuming at each reported failure; probably everyone in Israel knew of it.

After the third, he went himself, well surrounded by guards, I can hear his booming words when he came to the great well in Secu, *"Where are Samuel and David?."* Such anger and demand!

He was told they were in Naioth in Ramah. He went there. What came over him at that point? Possibly his unstable mind was caught up in the frenzy, or the spirit of God was there. Anyway, *"he too stripped off his clothes, and he too prophesied before Samuel, and lay naked all that day and all that night."* Was David doing the same, my David?

Papa as a sotted drunk, surely not looking like a king, some wondered if he too were among the prophets, *it is likely others wondered if he were out of his mind again.*

When he recovered, David had departed, joined by the messengers who had no place to go. David never will be alone for long, both men and women are drawn to him as moths to a flame, *to whom does my David play and sing?*

I feel the vibration of his strings in the long lonely nights, feel them picking up, wrapping, entwining night songs of crickets, softening the cry of jackals; nights are worst and best without David, and with David.

David no longer sends word to me, and I grieve, my days and nights are consumed with thoughts of him, with sadness that no issue came from our love. David is a beautiful boy, a fullblown man, no longer my David. ...

One day, he returned to Jonathan as though a repentant son, *"What have I done? What is my guilt? And what is my sin before your father, that he seeks my life?"*

Jonathan replied, *"Far from it! You shall not die. Behold, my father does nothing either great or small without disclosing it to me; and why should my father hide this from me? It is not so."*

David knew that Jonathan was expressing more hope than reality there. Nevertheless, he replied, *"Your father knows well that I have found favor in your eyes; and he thinks, 'Let not Jonathan know this, lest he be grieved,' But truly as the Lord lives and as your soul lives, there is but a step between me and death."*

Knowing he was right, Jonathan responded, *"Whatever you say, I will do for you."*

What do you see in these words of the future king, has he moved aside? Evidently things went on without my knowing, since I had been cut off from the inner circle, because David said: *"Behold, tomorrow is the new moon, and I should not fail to sit at table with the king; but let me go, that I may hide myself in the field till the third day at evening. If your father misses me at all, then say, 'David earnestly asked leave of me to run to Bethlehem his city; for there is a yearly sacrifice there for all the family.' If he says 'Good!' it will be well with your servant; but if he is angry, then know that evil is determined by him. Therefore deal kindly with your servant, for you have brought your servant into a sacred covenant with you. But if there is guilt in me, slay me yourself; for why should you bring me to your father?"*

Why David would think he should sit at table with the king when the king is seeking to kill him is puzzling. Custom says to be in attendance, but it does not say to put your head on a block when putting it there gets it chopped off, common sense says that, some of which David has, as well as beauty.

I am hurt that David is avoiding me, if he can see Jonathan, he could see me. Possibly he has tired of me, possibly? Is it possible papa is leaving me free as bait to lure David into danger and David knows? Am I a goat to be tethered out as bait for the lion? *My life has come apart.*

Some time ago, I remarked about the comfort of having God as our king; if only it could be so again, since papa was chosen, we've seen little comfort.

At first he was humble; it seemed good to have a king among us available for personal viewing, one with our own strengths and failings, those of all Israel. Now, mostly we see his failings, they loom so large his strengths are forgotten. *Oh for God's presence as it once was.*

Why do I tell you these things? I must talk to someone; since you're available and willing, you're chosen. No, it isn't that simple ... I'm lonely; papa has isolated me; David makes no effort to see me; even Merab is gone to her marriage and not available to hear my cries, Jonathan is friendly but busy and no longer needs my company. My only vocation is seeking information about David – *and worrying.*

If only I had a child by David, if he would see me once more, God might bless our union. I will ask Jonathan to speak to David about me; surely there is reason for his neglect. I felt no lessening of interest in our time together; no whisper came of other women, I was his only love interest, but I must be practical: a man alone too long grows lonely. It's time he came back to me if only for a secret visit, but he does not, and he could, he could, I know he could.

"You're being foolish, Michal', David is out of favor, to bring him here would make it worse for you and put him in danger, forget the thought."

"Have you not mentioned me to him when you've been together?"

"We've not had time for anything but the most essential, besides, your cause was lost when you deceived papa, it's no use."

"I'll find another messenger."

"No one will risk Saul's anger for you, Michal', come to reality."

He was wrong; I found one, the first one I asked. For a fat fee, he promised to get a message to David. The message was simple, "I need to see you before I'm further isolated."

Nothing came of it except the fee went into the thief's pouch, likely he never spoke to David; if he had, David would have come to me. He said he gave David the message, he lies.

How can I survive?

I will survive by following David's trail through reports that come to the court; if you're interested, we'll follow together. Who can tell what fate (or God) has in store for us? Knowing David, our time will not be dull – unless my concern with my future interferes too much.

CHAPTER V
FOLLOWING DAVID'S TRAIL
as he runs from Saul and battles Philistines.

Is this a story of things past? I become so involved in the telling that it joins today, you will forgive me as I slip in and out of these experiences already gone, at times in their midst again, it is impossible to recount them without doing so.

David is a beautiful man, yes, I said that before, several times, this time I'm speaking about his spirit. He loves me, I know he does. Papa Saul has caused us trouble, but David will come back to me.

The whispers about his philandering? Any virile man would seek company after so long a time, I will not hold that against him. That is the lot of women, is my mind slipping?

Papa has not forgiven me for helping David when the guards came for him, I thought he would eventually. That he hasn't may be a sign of worsening insanity, always before, his spells would weaken and our trust would resume. Thus far, no sign of forgiveness....

God be with me, and with David, no one else can intervene.

Surely David could find a means of getting to papa, no, Saul is king with heavy guard, David must run or hide....

"Then said David to Jonathan, 'Who will tell me if your father answers you roughly?'

And Jonathan said to David, 'Come, let us go out into the field.' so they both went out into the field."

As you see, they continued to see each other in the very worst of conditions, surely David could have found means of sending word to me.

How do I know all that was said between them in private? It is much later, conditions have changed several times; we will speak more about that as our saga unfolds or unravels, as you might say.

Jonathan held to his love for David, protested faithfulness when David expressed worry about it, and promised to tell David if Saul planned good or bad for him.

David used that love by tugging on Jonathan's emotions until Jonathan made him swear again his love for him. So much is wrapped in that thought: David's uncertain position, his uncertain thoughts, worry about that which had been promised him by God, concern that Jonathan would turn on him at this time of trouble. David proved human in this time, yes, and time again.

How wrapped up in each other they were, David and Jonathan, almost as a love affair, yet not at all, for both had eyes only for women as far as I have known.

In reflection, Jonathan has never discussed that with me, one of the few things we've not talked about, I do know he has his own wife and children though they don't loom as large to him as to some.

David? I am sure he is not interested in boys.

Strange that I should mention that, though it may be on my mind because of my concern for David's affections, papa asked long ago if I did not know about men's intimate opportunities. Of course, those things are discussed among women, what else is available to them? Even at that tender age, a female is a woman, should we talk about camels and asses, of wars, of work in the vineyard?

We talk about men, their loves, their doings, relationships of every nature come in for attention sooner or later, by the age of puberty, a maid knows about life, even if only from conversation. Do men speak only of war and crops? Highly unlikely, I would say.

Now I think about David and wonder if he thinks about me. There is no indication he does. Mainly, reports come in of his zigzag path as he evades Saul's agents, with some talk of other interests, those depress me.

I was not there, but, as papa held council, as usual, he looked for David in his customary place ... '*as usual*'? Yes, as his fashion of late, his madness dominated. Madness threw a scattered pattern in papa, his people. Only a mad man would send agents to kill a subordinate and then expect him to present himself at next council. Papa did that, and no one was surprised.

Little did he understand his power, or his own mind, when

Israelites shouted praise to David's victories, papa trembled and fumed. He did not understand that not even David, who killed Goliath, could take his throne until God withdrew his hand.

(Thoughts are a strange field. *Where an ass and a lion live together in close habitation, peace has no fodder* – has someone said that before? Papa was the cause of that thought, yet, after saying it, I realize many of us feed from the same field ... it may fit us better than him.)

When Saul asked Jonathan why David was not at council, Jonathan made up a story that only kindled papa's anger. "David earnestly asked leave of me to go to Bethlehem; he said 'Let me go; for our family holds a sacrifice in the city, and my brother has commanded me to be there. So now, if I have found favor in your eyes, let me get away, and see my brothers.' For this reason, he has not come to the king's table."

Papa's thinking often was confused, frequently without reason, yet at times his insight was piercing. Finally the jousting for position ended, *this time his insight was true.*

Papa said to Jonathan, *"You son of a perverse, rebellious woman, do I not know that you have chosen the son of Jesse to your own shame, and to the shame of your mother's nakedness? For as long as the son of Jesse lives upon the earth, neither you nor your kingdom shall be established. Therefore send and fetch him to me, for he shall surely die."*

Yes, papa now used mama as an excuse for many things, even involving her shamefully in this tirade. *Men have strange minds, even family privacy is cast into the wind and blamed on women.* She did not deserve that, surely God will hold him accountable.

David could not or would not unseat King Saul, but Jonathan's kingdom would never come to pass with David overshadowing him. I don't know if Jonathan understood the truth of papa's statement, if he did, either his love for David or honor binding his pledge of brotherhood was greater than his desire to be king.

There will never be a closer tie than between those two – *in the end profiting only one. Who but God knows if it was the right one.*

"Then Jonathan answered Saul his father, 'Why should he be put to death?'"

"But Saul cast his spear at him to smite him; so Jonathan knew his father was determined to put David to death."

The attendants were agape, frozen, unable or afraid to move between them.

This time, papa's anger exploded on Jonathan, first son, heir to the throne, his longtime favorite. Did he really intend to kill with his thrust? Thrusts in anger usually mean what appears. Uncontrolled fury is without reason or plan; so it was with papa this time.

This outraged Jonathan so much he stormed from the table without taking food. The next day, he went to David and told him what awaited him at the hands of Saul if he tarried.

Again Jonathan swore loyalty to David and parted.

What of my repeated assurances that papa's and Jonathan's trust remained constant? There was this interruption; it could have been permanent. A remnant of love, sanity, or a memory blank opened the path between them again, still papa and Jonathan were one.. Did I not tell you, males are favored without reason, except that God gave them the form? It is so, but I did not hold it against Jonathan. Or did I?

CHAPTER VI
MICHAL''S FATE IS DECIDED

It is time to tell what happened to me: You have heard my worry that David has made no attempt to communicate with me, you've heard about my isolation in the house of Saul. My life has changed greatly, as has that of David. Now my life would change even more, never would I have foreseen what papa was to decide.

He gave me to Palti of Gallim for wife, he did, though I am a married woman.

My reaction was dismay, then refusal, a useless gesture. I should have expected something like this after what he did to Merab for less cause, it says something about papa's ingrained sinews about even his own spawned. The male may be forgiven disloyalty, not so the female. Sons are also favored above his wife; she was the vehicle for providing male heirs. I'm digressing again.

Papa would not listen to my plea for leniency, his decision was final, no room for change....

After our earlier break, I wondered how I could survive. That was a picnic under an olive tree compared to this. Papa would not let me argue with him, so I argued with myself, I schemed, I devised a hundred ways to get out of the order; all wasted.

Often I had thought of Papa's lack of constancy; this time there was no wavering – it became his long suit.

I would send word to David, no, I would not send word to David. Of what use would that be when he makes no effort to see or communicate with me?

"Take this message to Saul for me, 'I love you, papa, it was because of fear I did that. I was afraid of what you would do because I let David go without telling you.'"

"It's no use, mistress, Saul warned us of your likely efforts to use us as tools to get what you want. He says you have no loyalty, one who takes that message to Saul will lose his head."

"Have you seen disloyalty in me? Am I not your friend of many years?"

"You look the same, but Saul's words make you a different person."

Saul's words made me a different person to everyone around me, and to myself. How can one be the same when terror rules the spirit, when gloom walks trails of the mind, when pathways to love and loyalty have been severed?

David is no use to me, because he is consigned to flight. I dreamed he would return for me, that we might run together, that in terror I could again share his bed; it was one more flight of fancy. My husband is gone from me, I must find my own way. I'm in the pit of hell – if mama would come to me, hold me, *oh, how I love mama.*

Why would a man take a woman for wife who does not want him for husband?

Palti accepted me not knowing my wishes; I was not consulted and had not seen him until the wedding. Would that I had the courage of Merab, she of such transparency.

What kind of bargain papa offered him I know not. Had he seen me? I don't know, would it have made a difference? Probably not, I'm still attractive to all men except David, evidently, even had I been ugly it may have made no difference.

What makes a man want a woman, a particular woman? Maybe the thought of having David's wife titillated his desires, maybe, maybe, maybe; what difference does it make? I am his wife, I accept his passions, I am no longer David's.

Am I committing adultery? When one doesn't have a choice is it sin? Will I have his children? Will I love them even though I don't wish to have them?

Where is the God of justice, of mercy? Where is God? Where is help? There is none, I am Palti's wife, David has forgotten me.

Finding new routines, patterning new thoughts, learning to accept defeat, these are my duties, in the midst of those I will follow David's doings as news drifts our way. No longer will court gossip go by me in my isolation. Now it will come to me as to all those not close to the court.

That does not mean no news, nothing is more talked about than David's activities, whether leading in war, running from Saul's men, or whispers of his women. *Yes, there is such talk, too much.* Sly comments within my hearing, about his female companions, reveal jealousies never suspected when he was with me, usually couched in words of sympathy for me, such as: "You'd think he'd have more respect for his wife than that, but that's like a man. You can't blame the woman; who wouldn't want him?"

Remember when we talked of not knowing where Meholah is? Do you know where Gallim is? It doesn't matter either, the thing of importance to papa this time is that I am properly punished for aiding David, for turning on papa. He pondered over it long enough; was it because it took that long to come by the punishment he wanted, or because he wanted me to stew in my nauseous juices? Living in vomit would have been no worse – sometimes it was, of a sudden retching.

Must I explain the punishment again? We will pass it by; you've heard enough for now, details will grow as we continue.

About Jonathan's relationship with papa; in spite of their falling out, something remained to unite them. Evidently, being heir to the throne made a difference, angry as both papa and Jonathan were, both were willing to find a way around their problem. Jonathan's loyalty was more with papa than with me in the end, probably more with David than with me, also.

A prick of doubt continues in my mind about Jonathan's desire to assume the crown when Saul dies, it is either that or he believes David has been chosen.

Their love is uncommon – that again.

CHAPTER VII
MORE OF DAVID'S SCRAMBLING

Are you ready to return for a time to David's scrambling? He may not have been frightened, but he scrambled, yet, always he found ways of more than surviving. Have you wondered where he gained sustenance?

When he left Jonathan, no one accompanied him, he who had commanded thousands. Even though unaccompanied, he had little problem finding lodging and food along the way. *Anyone approached almost fainted at the opportunity of assisting the great David.* (You can imagine, he soon was not traveling alone.)

He could have anything in the household, what he took other than food and lodging, I know not. I would like to believe he minded his manners, though, of course, he did not.

Directly he went to Ahim'ilech, priest at Nob, there he put together a story about the king sending him on a secret mission known to no one; of how he soon would meet and keep an appointment with some young men who needed food.

Significantly, Ahim'ilech was seen to tremble when David approached.

(All this was seen and heard by Saul's chief herdsman, Do'eg the Edomite, who was detained there – it was reported by him in due time.)

Apparently what David came for was Goliath's sword that was stored in the priest's care, food was the small-talk used to approach the main interest, though not without importance itself. Goliath's sword, who but David would think to wield it in battle, successfully? Only confidence of success would tempt one to reach for it, none but David did that.

The first concern of Ahim'ilech was that the young men who

would partake of the holy bread must have kept themselves from women, in other words, holy ... how little it takes to be holy, in the view of some.

How can women feel worthy within these belittling beliefs? On the other hand, some time ago papa and I talked of the prostitutes that follow armies ... if interpreted properly, this restriction to be holy could result in benefit to women, at the cost of men's comfort, possibly, even, at the cost of recruits for the armies.

David often assured me that his men refrain from women when on a mission, even a common mission ... such holy zeal from a man of David's avid interests! If true, if only it pertained now!

(Do my observations divert your attention from main issues? They are my way of coping. I hope you will humor me.)

David carried away the bread and Goliath's great sword, *thereby assuring the death of Ahim'elech,* bowing to David's wishes often proved more costly than appeared on the surface, it was so for Ahim'elech.

My own life sometimes appears to be a similar sword. You do not see the comparison, you say David married me? In the long run, his concern was for his interests, not mine, would I have denied him his interests? Not likely, actually, my interests were akin to his in some respects.

From there, David escaped to seek shelter with A'chish, king of Gath, enemy of Israel, that lasted only until the people of Gath began the chants about Saul killing his thousands and David his ten thousands.

With that, David, in desperation, feigned madness, fearing A'chish would retaliate for his earlier victories against them. *At last David may have reached real terror.* His ploy to get away worked only when spittle ran down his beard, then A'chish wanted nothing more to do with a madman.

Once again David ran in desperation, now to the cave of Adullam. Were words of his troubles circulating at the time? Oh, yes, though they were spotty and not all true. When he came in contact with people, word of his doings traveled quickly, few could resist boasting of seeing the great David, slayer of Goliath and the tens of thousands, also the fugitive, still beautiful, still wearing the halo, worshiped by men and women alike. Few believed he was running in terror, the killer of Goliath run in terror? Not possible, fair David would not run in terror.

While David ran from Saul, I lived with Palti as his wife, though I was the wife of David. Can a woman be married to two men at the same time, is that bigamy? Then why is it not bigamy for men?

I have begun to worry because again I have not conceived, you thought I did not wish children by Palti ... that was my wish, though somewhat it has been modified. Why? It confirms that which I would not accept: it was I, not David, at fault for our childlessness, a child, even Palti's child, would give me joy for living – and pride in being a normal woman. You thought I did not wish to be a normal woman?

It is clear that Palti has come to love me, that is both good and bad, good in that he is kind to me, bad in that I want David, you thought I was over that? Never will I get over wanting him.

Sadly, Palti knows of my persistent love for David. It is impossible that he not know, my moods swing up and down with news of David's troubles; only an ox would not see it.

Palti is no ox, David is the ox.

When David escaped, he went to the cave of Adullam, where his parents and brothers and all their retinue joined him, finally, you see, his brothers have joined his leadership. From necessity, or willingly? Likely of necessity, being the brothers of fugitive David is no blessing. Being the parents is no better.

You wondered if stories of his whereabouts were known? This will answer your question: while he was staying at the cave, four hundred men joined him, and he was their captain. Four hundred, coming singly or in small groups, do not find one unless his whereabouts are known.

He could have had four thousand, but that would have brought instant conflict with the army of Saul, as well as multiplied difficulty in securing provisions ... you're aware that four hundred men soon bring women, families ... you thought these would sacrifice their comfort to follow David? What a simple thought, David's entire family was there, *except his wife*, possibly he didn't need her.

Who were they, these men? Men of debt, in distress, the discontented, these became his army. His army was small and nondescript, but he was no longer alone. *Of course David's family joined him, they were in grave danger now that David was truly fugitive,* Saul's vengeance well might be vented on them, or, he could take them and use them as hostages to control David. David knew that, he was only partly stupid ... there!

With four hundred, David must move or face Saul's legions. His mother and father were left in the care of Mizpeh, king of Moab, while he ran. Then, on the advice of the prophet Gad, David went into Judah, into the forest of Hereth. Yes, his brothers were with him, though they may not have wished to be. How it must have galled them, taking orders from his subordinates – the brother they bullied as a child.

Now if four hundred found David, Saul would find him. So it would seem; yet papa's people loved David, withheld information of his whereabouts, papa knew that, he was not without guile, though sometimes stupid.

When news came of David's doings, papa made fun of his servants who trusted David, who conspired to keep news from their king. He shamed them until one reported the story of Goliath's sword, of how it was given to David by the priest Ahim'elech. You may have one guess as to who reported: *Of course it was Do'eg the Edomite who had been on the scene and witnessed the event,* that assured death to the holy man who had believed, at least accepted, David's made up story.

It was then papa called Ahim'elech in to challenge him for assisting David, for giving him provisions and Goliath's sword, *there he accused him of conspiring against his king.* Likely papa saw the sword as David did: a rallying symbol for increasing David's support among the Israelites, as though he needed it after his continuing victories – the common people saw him as a golden wraith leading an army of wraiths, not possible of capture or defeat. Even the lowest elements of papa's army who fled to David prized that image-cloak and became good soldiers.

Ahim'elech was no coward. He replied with vigor, he challenged Saul that David had all the rights of son-in-law of the king, of captain over his bodyguard and one honored in the king's house. He denied knowledge of any plot against the king, you see, even Ahim'elech the priest recognizes me still as David's wife.

His words were, "And who among all your servants is so faithful as David, who is the king's son-in-law, and captain over your bodyguard, and honored in your house? Is today the first time that I have inquired of God for him? No! Let not the king impute anything to his servant or to all the house of my father; for your servant has known nothing of all this, much or little."

The priest was as innocent of guile as most others in the kingdom, few saw the ambitions that coursed through the great veins in that virginal-looking David head. Simplicity and wishful thinking controlled a people longing for innocent purity of heart in their leader, in David they saw innocence and purity, apparently, too, wished him their leader.

Papa knew their thoughts, knew Ahim'elech's adulation. Nothing would have calmed papa that day, when his guard would not kill the holy man as ordered, he commanded Do'eg, the Edomite, to do so. Without scruples to detain him, Do'eg commenced the butchery. When he finished, eighty-five holy priests who wore the linen ephod were dead.

But he was not finished; once begun, his enthusiasm mounted as he continued – without hindrance from papa, *"And Nob, the city of the priests he put to the sword; both men and women, children and sucklings, oxen, asses and sheep he put to the sword."*

Truly, David's actions did not bring good to everyone, have you forgotten it was David who started the chain of this sad tale? Without papa's order, it would not have happened, without Do'eg, it would not have happened, without David's use of Ahim'elech, it would not have happened. Without David....

Ahim'elech performed his last sacrifice, himself the offering, adding to it everyone in the city of Nob, garnishing the act with common animals mingled with slain children ... who gets credit for this carnage? The Philistines were not involved.

David's made-up story to Ahim'elech the priest signaled the end for the innocent one and hundreds of other innocents, some say three hundred eighty-five. Are they numbers or men, women, boys and girls, babies, who hurt, who were murdered for no cause except to see them bleed and die?

Who was blessed or benefitted by their fear, their deaths? Do'eg? Papa? One holy man's mistake stimulated anger beyond measure in papa, or was it lust for killing that was stimulated?

Where was God while his holy ones were put to the sword, while their blood drained? While they called for mercy, *even the children?* Those are questions beyond any persons's answering, only God can answer in His own time.

Will there be a time when love reigns over hate, when wickedness falls before weakness, when the beauty of God shines to all people, when the poor in heart and body find strength outside their frailties? Will there come an aqueduct for God's ministrations to his people? David says there will be such a time.

One named Abi'athar escaped the slaughter and fled to David for safety, there he told David what had happened. David said, *"I knew on that day, when Do'eg the Edomite was there, that he would surely tell Saul. I have occasioned the death of all the persons of your father's house. Stay with me, fear not; for he that seeks my life seeks your life; with me you shall be in safekeeping."*

'Fear not,' he said? Would anyone trust David again?

Nothing seemed to shake their confidence that David would save them from whatever chased them, the people of Nob died in result of David's action. Did that affect their confidence in David? It was as though it did not happen.

With this began David's ascent from the depths. The next news of David that came to us recounted an incredible tale, details came later; since I now know them, they will be included.

At first we could not believe what we heard, David with his small motley army had attacked the Philistines, who were attacking Kei'lah, robbing the threshing floors.

(How these former sea people had adapted to land warfare. What warriors they were – those who, like our people, were invaders from another land, they from the north by sea, Israelites from the east by land; both claiming this land to be their home, both signing boundaries with their mark, willing – eventually, eager – to kill entire peoples including babes to hold the land now claimed as their own. Of course there was a difference, God had given us the land, unfortunately he did not make that clear to the Philistines. Why did he not tell them? I don't know; it could have saved much killing.)

Out of this came a victory in the miraculous, victory for David's ragged army that at first refused to fight. According to the story, *twice the Lord told David to attack before his men would follow,* like nothing else, this should prove David human: his men trusted him but could not bring themselves to face the enemy, not even when David promised them God's help. What a disappointment it was to David to see his army melt into the hills when he ordered attack!

When they realized their alternatives, in the night they returned to camp sheepishly in small groups. David sat quietly gazing into the campfire, waiting until a great group assembled, shifting nervously before him, awaiting his attention. Before he allowed them food and rest, they must swear obedience to his orders, even in the face of odds. Again, he promised them God's protection – he did not say if for every soldier, or only for David.

Nevertheless, it happened again, how much more difficult to face him again around the campfire in the night, I feel David's despair as he sits alone gazing into the lonely flames, wondering if they will return, if ever they will show courage, follow his orders. What did he say to them this time?

When finally they took action, they slaughtered the mighty Philistines and took their cattle. This time news reached papa as quickly as us, it included information of David's whereabouts in Kei'lah.

Papa said, *"God has given him into my hand; for he has shut himself in a town that has gates and bars,"* immediately he called his troops to take David.

After that would you expect people of Kei'lah to turn hero David over to Saul? *"Everyone was ready to assist the great David,"* isn't that what I said? Everybody, that is, except the people of Kei'lah, their envy surfaced.

David suspected their loyalty, else why would he have inquired? *"They will surrender you,"* is what David heard from God when he inquired through the *ephod brought by Abiathar the one who escaped from Do'eg's slaughter at Nob, who still trusted David more than any other.*

With his army, now six hundred, David again escaped, this time to strongholds in hill country of the Wilderness of Ziph. I could have made it easier for him by taking the worry of running the camp, or is another who follows doing that for him? How do they occupy themselves if not the usual camp duties?

Word is that David finally was afraid, because the armies of Saul gave no respite from the chase. *I've changed my mind. I do not believe it!* He may be cautious, but not afraid. He was not afraid of Goliath, why would he be afraid of crazy Saul, not afraid of the one papa would not face, the one David purposely angered with his sling?

Evidently Jonathan believed, because he went to David in the wilderness to encourage him to trust God. Jonathan had no trouble finding him. Now my question has been answered. Jonathan does not want to be king. These are Jonathan's words, *"Fear not; for the hand of Saul my father shall not find you; you shall be king over Israel, and I shall be next to you; Saul my father also knows this."*

Of course they knew, and I knew, though I would not admit it for fear of admitting disloyalty to my favorite brother. Somehow, Jonathan knew what David had long known. Who but Jonathan would know and still love his friend? Who but David would know and use the one he would supplant, his friend, play on him as on strings of the lyre?

Repeatedly David made Jonathan declare his loyalty. Compare the two, Jonathan's pledge of loyalty to David: David's pledge of love to me. Who held true?

A woman's name has been linked with David's for some time now. She apparently goes to him when he is settled in one place. *That is it, he has been alone too long. I will go to him in the wilderness. No, he is not exactly alone, but he has only one wife, that is I.... He needs me.*

I ask you, is it fair that he must live alone? It would be too great a temptation for men of lesser hungers than David's.

What about Palti, what will I do about Palti? I will leave him here, or, if he likes, he can join David's army; new recruits are always welcome. Will I slip away without telling him my whereabouts? Of course not, I owe him more than that, Palti has been good to me – that David needs me is not his fault.

Palti insists on joining me, worrying that I will be in danger traveling alone.

"Michal', you do not think well. You wouldn't go a day's journey without being molested. Have you no understanding of men? Brigands are men, are they not? Think you not they could see through your disguise? Would you hide your voice? Does it have the sound of a man's? Where is your usual judgement?"

"Why do you worry about me when I leave you to hunt for another, Palti? Have you no pride? Any other man would say, 'Good riddance.'"

"You have poor judgement, your mind is addled, little one, I must go along to see you come to no harm."

"Come to your senses, Palti, I am not little and you have known long that my heart will never untangle from David, I came to you without pretense. Saul gave me away as punishment – your mind deserted you when you took me."

"It did, unfortunately, now there is no going back. You are my responsibility, Saul would kill me if I left you alone."

"I have never been your responsibility, until my heart loosens its tangles for David, I am his responsibility, though he does not accept it. And papa no longer cares about my welfare."

"In the absence of that, someone must care for you, little one. I shall go."

He is right, of course, even disguised as a boy, there would be great danger, disguising this body would be difficult, the voice more so. We will go at once. He persists in calling me "little one," he, too, has weakness of mind.

Our journey began well; news of David's hiding place was on every tongue, mostly in agreement one with another. Papa is out with an army after David again, David moves, Saul follows, always only a few arrows behind.

David's four hundred defeated the Philistines, his six hundred could defeat Saul's armies if God would go ahead of him. Possibly

God has not made up his mind which to support at this time.

Long ago, David showed his stature for kingship; through Samuel, God long ago said papa's kingdom shall not last. Will Jonathan precede him? It is possible – God allows Saul to continue, possibly he will grant Jonathan a term before David, even though against Jonathan's wish.

Saul's madness should abort him as God's anointed, will it be Jonathan or David who follows? Why has God not chosen to make the change? Why has God abandoned me?

You see no connection in these questions? Both affect my life, do they not? Were Saul out and David in as king, my lot could change ... would I overlook Jonathan, much as I love him? My mind jumps to David as a pigeon to its nest. Where is Palti in this ... he is a good man. Where is Palti in God's plans? There we get into questions that have no end. Palti is caught in the currents of others' lives, swept along without recourse, he is not alone in that.

Where are the multitudes being slaughtered in wars, do they matter to God? Sometimes it appears only the enemies of God's chosen people die in wars. (It now appears that I, too, am among his enemies.)

That is not so. Many, many of God's people die in carnage. Did not the priests slaughtered by Do'eg belong to God, where was God when Do'eg continued the slaughter even to women and children of the priestly families? God watched while Saul's orders were carried out and exceeded even to the children and animals of the innocent ones.

Does God have a place for those not of the chosen people, is it always his wish that they be slaughtered without mercy? Does he have some who may be slaughtered to the last person and others who are not to be touched? Who hears these messages of slaughter from God, do they hear right?

Those are other problems we will not solve this day; though continually we look to God for answers to questions beyond our minds, over and over I probe for the heart of God for children, for mercy, for justice sprinkled with kindness. In some measure, I see it in the depths of David, and then it is lost in his excesses. Even at his worst, a trace of God is in David, at his best he speaks for God, it is the mixture that confuses me, is there not one pure?

Somewhere one may be pure, unmixed; I will continue to seek, possibly we must escape to the heavens in search of God and love, there in the presence of God, there will not be feet of clay standing between us.... God himself will give untarnished light that all may trust.

Saul's bent toward killing frightens me, it is as though now he kills to satisfy a habit, a hunger as for food, possibly even as a substitute for sex now that he is older. It is time for God to turn over the throne to David. (Or should the last be a question, the other, also? Do I blaspheme, assuming to know more than God?)

I pause on that thought; beautiful David also has changed since being near the power circle, or since making his own.

What does God see when he chooses a king for his people? Is there none who will keep simple graces of heart?

Palti and I wandered through trails in the wilderness, searching for David and his army, anyone can point to David; he is that way; no, the other way. We crossed our own tracks several times, following directions of ones who knew his exact whereabouts,. "Oh, yes, a contingent of David's army went by only a few days ago, he is no more than a day's travel in that direction." And off we went, grateful to be so near our goal.

How can it be so difficult to locate an army? Everyone seems to know their whereabouts until we search for them, then they have flown to another place not yet known.

Saul, too, may be having the same difficulty locating him.

Palti has suggested another danger: what would papa do if we stumble into his camp by mistake? Palti is no ox, the only similarity is the gentleness attributed to the ox; Palti has that. His mind is as sharp as David's, though not as cunning or ruthless. I am sorry for Palti, caught against my love for David.

Have I offended you with negative comments about David, you would not describe David as ruthless? What of the slaughter of innocents, babes, when he plunders?

Certainly he chooses when and where – he is selective, usually it is the heathen who feel his sword, but not always, not always, if you watch, *you will see*. No matter, we will continue searching for David, *danger is no worse to me than rumors of David fathering a child by a concubine.*

There, it is said. Jealousy is in my mind as a burrowing canker, true or not, sitting idly by while that may go on is beyond me. It twists my mind against God, I will not accept that David would stoop to entertain a courtesan, he is above that. I don't mean to say he is not interested in women, certainly he is; but he would not involve himself in cattle-herd activities.

You do not understand the expression? I will not explain.

Now we have done it! Palti's fear came to pass; we stumbled into a scouting party from Saul's army, they have not recognized us. Palti is trying to brazen it out, claiming to be on a mission for God.

"Come clean, man, you are searching for the outlaw David to join his renegade band."

"Would I take my wife along to join an army? Your head isn't in its place." With his bluster he could have had truth in his carry-sack.

"Your horn isn't sounding true; we've seen you before, your trail strays as crooked as ours; you search for David also. Come, you'll account to king Saul."

As quickly as that, we came on bad times. My foolishness is beyond understanding; I am stupid, as well, I can't imagine papa's anger when we're taken to him with the soldier's good guess about our mission.

Were I alone, it would have fared worse for me, even had they recognized me, I might never have been taken to papa. I'm not sure which would be preferable. Yes, I am sure, I would rather face the men. That would not be pleasant, but I would recover, papa's killing angers frighten me beyond measure.

Do you think I exaggerate, that he would not direct it at me? Then you've not heard anything I've said in this story, has he not several times lunged at David with his spear? David who once was his favorite, do you think he was being playful?

Papa's killing is unhinged compulsion, it has consumed his reason, but not his craftiness, and God allows him to remain king of his people ... after sending word that he would not, if we were given the right message

"Well, Michal', they tell me you've taken your husband on a hunt for David and his renegades, you prefer him to your husband and your father? How is that possible, has he sent for you, has he told you how much he misses you? I had heard he is otherwise occupied."

"No, papa, David has said nothing to me, your soldiers have misinformed you, we are on a holy mission, as Palti told them."

"You have never bent toward holiness, Michal', your mind has many tracks, but that isn't one of them."

"I have turned to God for comfort since you gave me to Palti, papa, my life has changed."

"I'm sure your life changed, I saw to that, though you were the cause of it when you turned on me."

"Have you no forgiveness, papa? Would you not forgive me for trying to save my husband's life? David paid the asking price for me, I am David's wife."

"Giving you to David was a mistake, God forgives such mistakes. Palti is your husband, how he lives with you I do not understand, look at his countenance; he is not an animal without feeling. Take your husband home, woman; another appearance before me and you shall have a different fate."

With that, we were pointed toward home and released.

"Palti, it's unbelievable, he released us, told us to go home, we will continue our search for David."

"Surely I didn't hear correctly, did you say, 'We'll continue our search for David?' *If we stand before Saul again, he'll have us slaughtered.*"

"We expected that the first time, it didn't happen, why would the second be more frightening than the first?"

"Michal', you are going home, I'll not take another such risk."

"Then you may return alone. I came out to find David, I will find him, papa doesn't frighten me."

"You are a crazy woman, because of that, I must remain near to see you do yourself no harm, I am as addled as you; nothing else accounts for such action. Would you like to ask your father for provisions to continue the search? No? Then soon we must replenish what the ass carries. Armies find it easier to obtain stores from people of the land, even if the locals are short for themselves, they fear to refuse."

"You're a bear, you shouldn't have come with me, the ass would be better company."

"By now you would have had the company of many men; if that's your wish, have it so."

"No, no, you are a bit better than the ass, come along."

He's right again, if we're taken once more it will not go well with us. Palti is a strange one: I go to find David; finding David loses me to Palti; Palti goes along to do himself in.

What a hopeless situation! We will learn to be more cautious, neither of us wish to be in the presence of Saul again soon.

When finally we found David's men, it was too easy to be true, *they found us.*

"What are you doing? Going from Saul to David, carrying news between them?"

"I'm looking for David to join his army."

"Is that why Saul released you, so you could join with David to fight Saul, think you not we did not see you as you played your games?"

"It does appear odd, doesn't it, but we truly are looking for David that I may join him."

"David is not simple; he would have our heads if we delivered you to him after being released by Saul.

"My woman is looking for David, she once was his wife."

"Be on your way, man, you've lost your wits."

"Truly, it is so, take us to him, he'll tell you."

"Even if so, he has no need of her now, be off with you."

Our story was too mixed up for belief, we would not see David this time.

Sadly, we began the slow return walk with nothing to show except blisters and discouragement, we both with blisters, I with discouragement.

Palti expressed sympathy, though I suspect his truthfulness ... being on our way home we grew careless, unfortunately.

"We released you with orders to return home, now here you are wandering as before; you appear to want another audience with the king. Fine, you may have it."

"No, no; on our way we became confused, please, let us continue, can't you tell we're headed away from the wilderness?"

"Except for that, you would see Saul, if we catch you again, you have fashioned your own execution sword; Philistine smiths could do no better.

"If you catch us again, we deserve what we get."

We went on our way, wrapping new blisters in leaves, coaxing the ass to move as we moved, it protesting, liking it no better than we and no better fed.

Once again I am doing the routines of wifery: cleaning, making bread, carrying water, visiting at the well, washing clothes, sleeping with Palti, mostly dull routines, but not all.

Palti has resumed his duties at the pottery shop, something he does with taste and pride. His legs are strong and his hands rough, though gentle.

I listen for news of David as always, yes, we continue to hear news almost more quickly than when we wandered about searching for him, that makes sense in that here we're known and trusted, people talk to us because we're no threat to them.

Me they trust because they know I'm out of favor with Saul. They fear him greatly, would say nothing to me if there were danger their words would be carried to him.

Here, I'm not thought of as King Saul's daughter, I'm a simple housewife, one of them, strange, strange, God has twisted my fabric to his whims.... Palti says God would honor honest questions.

"Why do you distrust God so, Michal'?"

"What makes you think I distrust God?"

"You're afraid he'll not like you because you question."

"I'm afraid my doubts will turn God's face from me, what if he approves the things I question? The killing of innocents, breaking the Commandments by his appointed, questioning as I search for a gentler God; when I see his spokesmen as equally good and evil as others, when I question that sometimes they have rubbed oil into their own skins to the loss of others."

"Have you considered that God may agree with you? Those he works with may not be perfect, give God as much room as you give yourself."

CHAPTER VIII
DAVID AGAIN MEETS A GIANT

Saul is no longer the hero; however, he is king, and power is with the king, good or bad, he knows that as do the people, though periodically he forgets. They asked for a king and got him, as for the king being my papa, I didn't ask for that. But in the end it is the same – we make the best of what we have.

At last it appeared Saul would catch David through the assistance of some who sold out to the king. *"Saul went on one side of the mountain, and David and his men on the other side of the mountain; and David was making haste to get away from Saul, as Saul and his men were closing in upon David and his men to capture them, when a messenger came to Saul saying, 'Make haste and come; for the Philistines have made a raid upon the land.' So Saul turned from pursuing David...."*

After that close call, papa likely expected to take David easily when he returned to the chase, it didn't happen. Papa went into a cave to relieve himself, lay down for a sleep, David waited, then went in and cut off the skirt of papa's robe, kind, merciful David would not attack the anointed king.... *But he would taunt him with his mercy.*

"See, my father, see the skirt of your robe in my hand;" and he made his goal clear, as though it had not been so since he was told of God's hand on him years ago. Why would he forget such a thing as that, told to him long ago before the man servant brought him to Saul's tormented attention?

"May the Lord judge between me and you, may the Lord avenge me upon you; but my hand shall not be against you...." What wisdom, what guile! His goal is clear, waiting for God's hand is

David's plan, that he waited so long to acknowledge his expectation is surprising. Everyone, including papa, already knew, it required amazing self-control to contain this incredible message so long, an amazing mind as well.

And David continued to hold his sword away from King Saul, easily David found Saul, easily passed the guards into the cave. Yet Saul chased David in endless frustration, it appears God opened one's eyes and blinded the other.

Had David been playing games with papa when he ran away? I doubt it, more likely the game was real, had papa caught him, he would have died, and Jonathan would have become king, like it or not.

Long since had papa forgotten the meaning of mercy, one killing thirsted him for another, and that for another. Slaughter had become his habit – human beings, men, women, children, babies, animals, anything that bled.

What can be so fascinating about humans bleeding, is the pleasure in watching life drain out of beauty? Can it be jealousy of others who have what he has lost, (Little has he lost, except peace.) or is it his expression of power, or another not yet mentioned?

In the early years, he talked as though carnage distressed him, "It bothers me, daughter, that children must suffer the sword for their parents' evil, but God knows, else why would he lead us to victory? I will never get used to it."

"I know, papa, you're a tender man, on your own you would stop before it gets to children." ...and then he might have; or he might not have, at a later date, it would be hard to imagine it was not done from his heart.

Am I saying that David's heart was different than papa's about killing? No; pointing out the absence of mercy in our doings – except where there was advantage to the mercy giver.

From the moment he cut Saul's skirt, it was clear who had won, David declared his victory when he told papa Saul the simple story by quoting "*'Out of the wicked comes forth wickedness'; but my hand shall not be against you....*"

Papa accepted defeat though yet in the future, with these words:

MICHAL'

"you are more righteous than I; for you have repaid me good, whereas I have repaid you evil.... I know that you shall surely be king." He also accepted that his king-line would not continue after himself, that Jonathan would not be king, gall was in his mouth billowing forth in clouds of bitterness clothed in honey – Saul's words but not his heart speaking.

Long since had David learned not to taste honey from Saul's lips, sometimes it clung to a spear.

For some time now, we have dealt only with David's and Saul's problems because to interrupt the telling would have spoiled your thought.

CHAPTER IX
DAVID'S WOMEN

Now we turn to the other matter, David's women, of whom I was first, as far as I know.

You note the worm that eats me, my inability to accept that David will have other women. *Why has God done this to me?* If men cannot be faithful, why, then, did he not make women able to tolerate their waywardness? Why must my stomach knot into spasms night after night when I lie thinking of David with another?

By this time, I should be adjusted to the fact that David is removed from me, that I have been put in the hands of Palti, gentle Palti. Palti, saddled with a woman who belongs to another. His life is as sad as mine.

Yes, I think of David when I should be thinking of Palti.

Do I belong to David? I did, yes ... with every caress, he assured me of his unending love. Is it possible David considers me soiled because of Palti? What of his women, that is different?

We have been apart for a long time now, is it reasonable to expect him to remain true to me? Possibly not reasonable, yet I expect it. He promised, what is a promise if not to be kept? Could he not have come for me? I could have traveled with him, others have.

How can he remain pure when they travel with him? His so-great-stories of abstinence when on a mission, where is God that he allows that? I did belong to him, but do I now?

As long as the prophet Samuel lived, David did not remarry. Now that Samuel is dead, the restraints are gone. Is my imagination speaking, or is it so? You decide.

MICHAL'

AB'IGAIL, Nabal's wife. No. 2., (Remember, I was first.)
"And Ab'igail made haste and rose and mounted on an ass, and her five maidens attended her; she went after the messengers of David, and became his wife.

"David also took Ahin'o-am of Jezreel; and both of them became his wives. Saul had given Michal' his daughter, David's wife, to Palti the son of La'ish, who was of Gallim."

In one stroke and then another David wiped me from his future as though we'd never known one another. I did not go to Palti of my own will, papa forced me, that didn't matter to David, it was as though he held me responsible, as though sleeping with Palti is something I chose. It is as if David felt released from me when I did that.

This amorous marriage coup of David's has moved us into another era, one that causes a change in my hopes. Now if I return to him I am not alone in his affections, I will share him with others. (Do I assume he was celibate these extended times apart? Of course not, but until now, he didn't marry again, now, one is not enough – was it ever?)

How shall I deal with that? *As though I ever will have opportunity to know.*

How did these instant marriages come about? Were they unrehearsed or well designed by David with help from his army commanders, did they get vicarious pleasure from entering into his illicit conquests? Illicit? Am I overstating the situation? I think not.

The details of Ab'igail's strategies are well known; it has the making of legends, few women in Israel's history have promoted themselves so cleverly and succeeded so completely.

On the surface, David appears innocent, but, I tell you, David was not as detached as he tried to appear. We will review the action; see if you agree with me.

Soon after Samuel died, David went to Ma'on where Nabal, the rich man, lived with his beautiful wife Ab'igail. David knew about Nabal, how he was churlish, about his wife's beauty, and their riches. He devised an elaborate plan clothed in a request for support for his rebel army, a request that he undoubtedly expected to be rejected. Why would he expect it to be otherwise? He told his men, " ... go to Nabal, and greet him in my name. And thus you shall salute him: 'Peace be to you, and peace be to your house, and peace be to all that you have.... Pray give them whatever you have at hand to your servants and to your son David.'"

His men conducted themselves with great care at Nabal's place in order not to jeopardize David's innocence. *'Give them whatever you have at hand?'* And you think he was innocent of the many faceted riches, the beauty, in that household?

Nabal rejected the request without hesitation.... David with four hundred men (or had he more now, it seems as though six hundred had joined him some time ago, no, at this time, four hundred, my mind is drifting) prepared to descend on Nabal to wipe them out, to slaughter Nabal and his men for refusing to support the rebel army.

"And David said to his men, 'Every man gird on his sword!' and every man of them girded on his sword; David also girded on his sword; and about four hundred men went up after David...." (There, four hundred.)

A wealthy, beautiful widow would have remained after the slaughter, a tempting partridge awaiting wooing, to see the strutting plumage of the male. Then came an odd twist when Ab'igail, without Nabal knowing, gathered supplies and took them to David, along with the supplies went a long speech taking on herself responsibility for Nabal's refusal and asking forgiveness, as, with great skill, she slipped in the hint about her surly husband.

It was a masterful speech, praising David's work for the Lord; nothing could have pleased him more. She ended by asking him to remember her when the Lord dealt well with him.

My inclination is to pass over her scheming speech with haste, but if we do that, you will miss feeling its brilliance, and David's eager response. Therefor, though it is not short, hear this:

"She fell at his feet and said, 'Upon me alone, my lord, be the guilt; pray let your handmaid speak in your ears, and hear the words of your handmaid. Let not my lord regard this ill-natured fellow, Nabal for as his name is, so is he; Nabal is his name, and folly is with him but I your handmaid did not see the young men of my lord, whom you sent."

How could she not see ten men at her own quarters, at least hear immediately about them from Nabal, would you not have reported to your wife such an incident with hero David's men?

Likely, it took a while to come up with a plan, when she did, it was a good one: "Now then, my lord, as the Lord lives, and as your soul lives, seeing the Lord has restrained you from blood guilt, and from taking vengeance with your own hand now then let your enemies and those who seek to do evil to my lord be as Nabal. And now let this present which your servant has brought to my lord be given to the young men who follow my lord. Pray forgive the trespass of your handmaid; for the Lord will certainly make my lord a sure house, because my lord is fighting the battles of the Lord; and evil shall not be found in you so long as you live. If men rise up to pursue you and to seek your life, the life of my lord shall be bound in the bundle of the living in the care of the Lord your God; and the lives of your enemies he shall sling out as from the hollow of a sling. And when the Lord has done to my lord according to all the good that he has spoken concerning you, and has appointed you prince over Israel, my lord shall have no cause of grief, or pangs of conscience for having shed blood without cause or for my lord taking vengeance himself. And when the Lord has dealt well with my lord, then remember your handmaid.'"

David saw her beauty, as though he hadn't already, forgave her for her husband's churlishness, and promised to grant her petition.

This woman of beauty was intelligent and crafty, as you see.

Was David susceptible, naive, or as crafty as she? Any would be as bad as the others in a future Israeli king – weak, stupid, or lecherously crafty. Read the story of his life and decide, read with a mind clear of Israeli' induced hero worship, see without drunkenness of the spirit – clear your mind. But I know that is impossible – the history of our people bends your thinking as it did mine.

When, on her return, Ab'igail discovered Nabal drunk at a celebration party, she had to wait to inform him of the problem she had created for him.

Later when Nabal heard about the meeting between his wife and David, his heart failed and he fell over with a seizure, soon to die.

The tale ends with David shortly sending soldier emissaries to woo Ab'igail to make her his wife, yes, my husband did that. She made haste, gathered her five maiden attendants and set off to accept his proposal, *as we knew she would.*

David was careful to see that the woman's marriage was severed before he became formally involved with her, he wanted no woman committed to two men, as I was when papa gave me to Palti. David wanted none of that, I could tell him, it doesn't work. Of course, he knows that from his own viewpoint, surely, he heard of my constant schemes to rejoin him.

You may search the story carefully without finding evidence of guilt on David's part to steal another's wife, his care was desert-dry-bone-clean in setting up Nabal for subsequent retaliation, actually murder, for denying the request; it was a plan worthy of a great general.

However, a similar experience later, *of which there is no doubt*, strengthens my guess of the lust planning by David. You will see.

Nabal almost escaped David's scheme when his wife, not knowing the plan, interfered, thereby stopping David's raid. Unfortunately (*for Nabal*) Nabal unexpectedly then caused an opening for it to work in a different way when his heart failed of fright, or anger. *Thereby, David was spared further scheming action or blame, by Nabal's timely death.*

Do you agree with my earlier question about David's guilt?

If there is still doubt, consider again when you hear related stories later in these memories.

AHIN'O-AM, No. 3.

At about the same time, David sent wooers to set up his marriage with Ahin'o-am, this confirms that he was in amorous pursuit of women at the time; remember, Samuel is gone.

I had not seen her, though we may assume she, too, is a beauty. David is not known for being attracted to unlovely women, some men are, but David wasn't among them, if without beauty, it was for political reasons.

I did not realize where this thought would lead: Possibly my statements about his attraction to me were founded on mistaken thinking. Without question, political ends were involved when papa offered me and he accepted – for both papa and David. Should I be included, also? And what of my belief that he appreciated my comeliness?

Will we assume, then, that he ignored those (political choice) wives in his nighttime activities? *An expression,* for he did not confine himself to nights in his activities, everyone knows he did not ignore even one of them, physical evidence of that exists.

Technically, possibly even legally, now he has three wives. And concubines?

The situation has changed, as mentioned earlier, but I do not agree that I am no longer David's wife, I have not given up my claim to him, granted, he shows no indication that he now considers me his wife.

Papa had a hand in all that when he sent me to the bed of Palti. For two who were once so close, papa and I have grown far apart. Men do not hesitate to take another man's wife. Yet if their own goes to another, under any circumstance of innocence, the wife is disqualified for her husband's bed ... I see no even justice in that, justice is not practiced or considered.

Is your mind bothered about speaking of marriage as going to one's bed? Shall we continue to hide the obvious, what is in the male mind at that occasion? Eating breakfast figs together, discussing the day's work ahead, daily devotions? Does religious fervor purify this zeal, change it to something different, at once become mentionable if assigned to God's wishes?

What causes David ... what causes men ... to want multiple women? To prepare his meals, mend his garments, care for his children? Yes, all of those. And, of course, the more obvious reason ... ignore it if you wish.

No, let's be honest with each other. Unless we are, this story will go untold and unheard – and a great segment of royal life will be left under the shadow of a bush. Or we could talk only of war and slaughter. If you would play such games with truth and reality, there is no use continuing. It is your choice, I will continue without you.

As David's story unfolds, it more and more takes on amazing similarity with that of king Saul: lust for power, lust for blood, lust for women, hunger for forgiveness.

That is not the picture of David you have seen and heard? If you are still here, did I not suggest honesty in our discussion? Repeating shibboleths will get us nowhere.

The one great difference between them now (papa and David), David asks forgiveness for his sinning (with women) and appears to believe his plea is granted, others, too, appear willing to grant his lusting as a forgivable, needful, part of his, of men's makeup. His comeliness provided a lure and forgiveness beyond the usual, from his countrymen.

I admit, he has not yet reached some of papa's excesses, in addition, at times he is made beautiful with a mixture of reverence and magnanimity that shadow the lusts. David, the shepherd boy, lusting?

At other times, he turns his ragged band loose on the defeated, slaughtering them to the last man and child, even so, he has not yet expressed papa's single-minded passion for blood – there is yet time.

His eye for women overshadows papa's already. Does God overlook, or allow that? What of the power hunger? It has taken root and shows promise of being healthy and strong.

David is a mixture hard to put in one container. *It is the differences from Saul that make people love him, not the similarities. Yes, they love him; very much they love him.*

Why do I love the two men who model all these things so well? Did I say I still love papa? If anything, I am inconsistent.

With such powerful motivation, why did David wait until Samuel died to launch into open flouting of morality in his lust for women? *Almost* open flouting, that is.

Even now, he continues to pay token respect to morality by trying to hide his schemes to obtain married women who please his eye. And, of course, he marries those he wants badly enough, that is the sure way to secure them for his attentions when desired. Although a well organized concubinage does the same thing, doesn't it?

I guess I really don't know why he chooses some to marry and not others, unless it is the woman's family place among people.

The question of why he waited until Samuel was dead? *Possibly because he feared the approval of God would be withdrawn, that bestowed by Samuel when David was in youthful innocence.* If so, it doesn't show great respect for the One God, taught by the prophets.

CHAPTER X
DAVID'S POWER AND MORALITY
His image was shielded

Saul with his great army continued to chase David with his small band of followers, as did I, both always a few steps late. Evidently David knew of my zig-zag efforts as well as papa's.
As David's confidence grew, he increased his risks almost to the point of foolishness.

From my words, you may have inferred that none remained in support of papa, that is not true, though David was widely popular.
Also, as long as Saul is king, he will have support, fear, and those currying favor ensure that. Support was divided and fluctuated back and forth.

Now the Ziphites came to papa, saying, *"Is not David hiding himself on the hill of Hachilah?"*
"So Saul arose and went down to the wilderness of Ziph, with three thousand chosen men of Israel to seek David...." You realize that is five times as many soldiers as David had.
David temporarily reversed from being the hunted to being the hunter, by cunning rather than power. He took his man Abi'shai with him at night, into the camp of Saul. Again Saul was at his mercy.... Practical Abi'shai wanted to kill Saul *and end the affair,*
"God has given your enemy into your hand this day; now therefore let me pin him to the earth with one stroke of the spear, and I will not strike him twice."
David would not allow it, easy as it would have been. In this he held to a moral position, *but not without other motives, also,* one he voiced: *"Do not destroy him; for who can put forth his hand against*

the Lord's anointed, and be guiltless?" Selfish or selfless morality? Instead, they took the spear and jar of water at Saul's head and slipped away without being detected, is there any wonder God loves David? Do my words reveal intimate knowledge and a bias toward David? When he told me this story, he told it that way, would you expect it otherwise?

You wonder how I got these things except from the mouth of David. How else would I know all the details? We will get to that in due time, with all my garrulousness, you may have detected that I am lonesome for someone to share with, as Jonathan, or even papa. I wonder if they miss our talks as much as I.

Palti does not have the interest or background for court discussion. Don't misinterpret that, Palti gets on with people, he is not without intelligence; but this is not about Palti, gentle, guileless Palti.

Further about David: he has a sense of beauty seldom found in a man. People are attracted to that, some see it as softness, often to their grief. I meant that in reference to words and language, though now that it is said, I realize it could as well refer to his appreciation of physical beauty.

His compassion to Saul when he had him at his mercy was for personal reasons. He seldom gave it to those who came under his heel in combat, except for his own ends. This was combat of a different level with different methods, sharply controlled by David's sure foreknowledge of what he was to be if God continued with him. Everything he did was with that in mind.

Where Saul slew thousands of Philistines, David slew tens of thousands. That was not done with tenderness or mercy. Slaughter is slaughter, killing and blood, regardless of the beauty or gentle image of the one who commands. Every person in Israel took note and sang songs around their thousands and tens of thousands, killing was the game around which legends were born, the national pastime, often blamed on the one spoken of in roundabout terms. Who do I mean? Who has been given credit? How often we lay on God our own excesses.

Was gentleness involved when he boldly loaded the stone to

smash Goliath in the forehead to begin the carnage? Well, at least, to carry it on.

And then when he coolly chopped off the giant's head and carried it by the hair *to be seen along the way,* and to show King Saul. He must have been aware of the pandemonium of awe he created as the cheering Israeli soldiers and civilians poured adulation on him, putting wings to his walk ... he knew, understood its precious value even in its first birthing.

What was the reason for his mercy to Saul? David also has a remarkable sense of tradition, of relationships of one thing or action to another, of the emotions created by one's bearing and of peoples' reactions. As acknowledgment of his attributes continue, his readiness for kingship becomes more obvious.

David has long known he will be king, he understands that how Saul is respected and treated will influence how he is respected and treated when he is king. He understands the value of traditions, that flouting them quickly destroys them.

By respecting Saul *as God's anointed,* he is encouraging respect for *the anointed king,* whoever it may be, but especially himself. He was setting precedent for his own treatment in due time, *is that clear to you?*

If I know David so well, why are we not together? Is that all that's involved, how about understanding myself? Why can I not be content with my lot in life, why do I long to be in the center of power when it is not the choice of a female to do?

Where were we in the tale of David's progress toward the kingship? Oh yes, he has spared Saul's life again but took his spear and jar of water. Is his motive clear? What has he done by sparing the king's life, yet proving he could have slain him but did not?

Was it done in secret and then forgotten? Oh, no! Immediately upon reaching safety, he called loudly to the army of Saul to taunt and point out his generous heart in allowing Saul to live, in returning good for evil.

His shouted speech ended with, "for the king of Israel has come out to seek my life, like one who hunts a partridge in the mountains."

MICHAL'

It was another of his masterful, veiled campaign speeches, making clear who is the man, who is master, who should be king – and of course he has already spared Saul's life, who can accuse him of plotting for the crown?

Papa Saul has not given up attempts at trickery. *"I have done wrong; return, my son David, for I will no more do you harm, because my life was precious in your eyes this day; behold I have played the fool, and have erred exceedingly."*

David answered, *"Here is the spear, O king! Let one of the young men come over and fetch it.*

"The Lord rewards every man for his righteousness and his faithfulness; for the Lord gave you into my hand today, and I would not put forth my hand against the Lord's anointed...."

These words if spoken only in Saul's hearing would have had one meaning; *but when shouted to the entire army, quite another,* anyone with perception would see that. But, of course, by now, the entire nation of Israel is ready to ascribe to David a halo, his public humility is astounding. I said *'ready to ascribe'*? He wears the halo they created; carefully tended and polished by the wearer and the creators.

Saul's reply should have reassured David, but it did not, David grew weary of flight from Saul's armies and went to Gath with his two (other) wives and six hundred men and their wives and children and all that went with them.

One wife has been forgotten. I, his first wife, remain with Palti. Yes, kind, gentle Palti.

Can you imagine David taking refuge among Israel's bitterest enemies, the perfect asylum? Probably Achish was as amazed as papa must have been, how Achish must have smiled when told of David's arrival seeking sanctuary from Saul.

I can hear him, "Welcome David, certainly, you may remain under my protection. I will provide you with a place to stay; Saul will not seek you here." Likely he chortled over this coup for days, weeks.

And Saul did not seek him there, possibly he has seen the end of David.

David humiliated himself once more when he asked, *"If I have found favor in your eyes, let a place be given me in one of the country towns, that I may dwell there...."*

Is this the man of character seen by Israel? Has fear found him? My pretended understanding of him is washed away; again, there is no predicting him.

No sooner asked than given, permanently given by Achish as a present.

I was not there, but I see here a city with all that six hundred men need to make and keep them satisfied for an extended period. Former malcontents do not suddenly become placid in isolation, not even with David as their leader, unless their needs are attended to.

This island of Israel in the midst of Philistia carried with it those necessities, some brought female companions, with men and women together come children, and all that goes with life for extended time. Those of David's men who did not bring women with them found them among the residents of the city as they could. David tried to stop that; he would tell you he was successful.

This was not a running wilderness camp, this was a city safe from Saul's army. Families formed, homes functioned, women cooked, brushed off flies, swatted mosquitoes, went to the well, gossiped, worried about tomorrow, spatted about their children's spats, threatened terrible punishment for mischievous behavior; endlessly, dogs barked, chickens scratched, outside and inside, birds sang and dropped their blobs on heads and backs, both men and women became involved in worrying out a living – for the long-time residents were loathe to feed them forever, especially for these enemy Israelis living among them.

Israelis among them were soldiers in training as well as farmers and herdsmen, tent makers and craftsmen of all kinds. Some began to learn metal skills from the Philistines, those who would share their skills – few indeed, for these Israeli intruders were held in suspicion. Their king, not they, had given their city to the enemy, now in their midst.

David kept his promise while there not to attack his hosts, time would show it did not apply to the distant future, when his great plans came to fruit. However, during this interlude, he attacked others as far away as Egypt – a violent interlude, indeed. For sixteen months, that went on, "and David smote the land, and left neither man nor woman alive." He may exceed papa in killing now, not commanded by God. Do you accuse me of prejudice when I speak so of him? You may verify my words if you wish.

The other side of David was clearly exposed during this sojourn. From time to time when David would return from a raid, Achish would ask, *"Against whom have you made a raid today?"*

David lied, beautiful David, man of God, did that? How can I say this about my David? *Because it's true, the record tells the story.* Shortly, you will see why I can talk about it now.

Has my truth turned you off? Are you still expecting the usual words of praise to hide cruelty, sordidness? Remember, you and I are much alike, though the halo I give David is bruised by broken promises, shattered by reality of which I'm a part.

Yours has been polished by legends, legends fashioned in the minds of a nation hungry for this beautiful man to fill their fantasies of the innocent-youth giant killer, they polish the halo with fervor not to be denied, and David deserves much adulation.

My fantasies are gone; lonely though it is, my love persists.

He claimed to be attacking his own people, Negeb of Judah, Negeb of Jerahmeelites, Negeb of Kenites – but, of course, did no such thing.

Instead, he continued his war practice on heathen people, had Achish known, the asylum may have been terminated at once. *You wonder how he could not have known? So do I, though, apparently, he did not.*

David killed everyone whom he attacked to prevent them telling what he did – how terrible (you were told of this earlier). I know, you do not want to hear these things about David, I would not say them, but they are true.

You know it is so, *our heroes are human; it isn't easy to accept. On the other hand, I love David and he has deserted me.*

"And David saved neither man nor woman alive, to bring tidings to Gath, thinking, 'Lest they should tell about us, and say....'" Yes, how terrible, David without compassion.

It lasted a while yet before David was again on the run.

I don't remember David lying earlier when we talked (I wince at the term). Or did he? Before going on a raid, he shared his plans with me, almost as an equal, as I told you, we shared more than the usual, that is my basis for continued hope that he was attracted to me, as he claimed – not won by diplomacy as sometimes enters my troubled heart, or is it mind?

How can he ignore me now, as though our sharing didn't happen? Wishfully, I keep forgetting he has two other beautiful wives now, and others, with little need of me. He is well cared for.

Once Palti and I searched for David without success, I long to try again, not so much with hopes that he will take me back, as that I may speak with him, probe his mind to see where he is now.

I know what you are thinking, "Where he is, is apparent from what he does. What could speak more clearly than his actions?"

True, yet it might clear my heart of longing for what once was. If not that, possibly it would give a clearer picture of his feelings in regard to me.

It would be cruelty to put Palti through that again.

CHAPTER XI
CHASING DAVID AGAIN, ALONE

My noble concern didn't last long, "Palti, I need to try again to see David."

"We've been through that, David has changed since you knew him."

"I know that, so have I. He still knows who I am – once he respected my thinking. The changes in him since Samuel died will bring no good to him or to Israel when he is king."

"You won't change him, Michal'. He isn't the innocent young man you knew, he is realizing the power of power."

"Did you say what you meant to say?"

"Yes, it happens even to one who becomes wealthy after knowing poverty, few can resist superior feelings, excessive display in some form. David is beginning before full power is his. Let him alone, don't break your head against a stone wall, I see my breath is wasted. I can't follow you forever in your pursuit-of-lost-dreams; you go alone this time, Michal'."

I saw his body sag, a tiredness rumple his face momentarily, seldom had I seen him so.

"I'm sorry, Palti, it isn't fair to you, but I must go."

"As you will, this time, you go without me."

Palti was wrong for once, traveling as a deranged, filthy beggar repels men, few look closely to see through my disguise.

If they recognize me as a woman, they have disgust that I am so unkempt. Such dishevelment arouses little interest of the dangerous kind, with an added stagger of confusion, it was near perfect, though travel was slowed.

From observation, I would have said some men will respond to any woman alive, it may not be so.

My chances of finding David are much improved without Palti, who would have thought it? Seeing David alone will free our conversation considerably. In my disguise, it will be no surprise if he throws me out, I will face that possibility when I see him.

Some still seek David to join his band, though he appears now to be limiting the number to six hundred, always, of course, there are losses from battle and sickness to be replaced. Few desert him, they have few choices except to join a band of brigands.

Papa's army is still about but not active in chasing David since he fled to live among the Philistines, papa may be as amazed as I at that turn of events. They seek him when he is out of his sanctuary, though he is in another direction – it is known he ventures forth.

From reports, papa's dementia has worsened, that has only increased his iron grip over the army. From the time of slaughtering the holy men and their families, fear has quieted complaints among his troops, unhappiness is there, but more cautiously displayed.

For those whose business is facing death, it would not seem they would fear death at the hand of their leader, but they do. The fist of Saul raised over them is more frightening than hoards of Philistines, more certain death. It is themselves they fear for now, rather than their oxen.

Even though danger of running over a band of papa's scouts is diminished, caution continues to be important. The Philistines, too, are a danger, bands of both continue to wander about, constantly a danger.

Again, it is no more out of my mouth than I walk carelessly into a group searching for David, will I ever learn?

"What are you doing here, crazy one?"

"What do you see, King David? I am here to guide your army."

"You are out of your head, woman, David needs none such as you, he would not feed you even for entertainment."

"I do not entertain, my directions from God are clear, I am to strengthen your army."

"Crazy women do not strengthen an army, he will chase you into the wilderness."

"No, he will hear my words from God or he will lose all he's gained. God does not toy with such as he, if you are not David, take me to him."

"How can we do that? We're looking for him ourselves."

"Then we will travel together, I have words from God for that man. No man can live with the Philistines and have the blessing of God."

"God speaks through holy men, old hag, don't lie about speaking for God. He will treat you as Saul treats those who lie to him, your tongue will be cut out."

"I know King Saul better than I know David, God has given me words for both, when I've spoken to them, they'll know the path of righteousness."

"Give us a sign that proves what you say, woman."

"You want a sign? You shall have a sign, I'll tell you the words of David when he ran from Saul into the wilderness."

"Only his wife or God would know that, and you're not his wife, what did he say?"

"He said, 'Let me go, why should I kill you?'"

"Either God told you or you have great wisdom. You may come with us as we search for David."

"Why do you go to him when he's given over to the enemies of God's people?"

"It's worse to be under Saul; he is mad."

"You're an honest man; Saul is mad, God withdrew his approval when he cast his spear at David, his time is short."

"What do they call you, old woman?"

"Michal' is my name, no other is important."

"The name seems familiar, though I know not where I've heard it."

"Names have little consequence unless they are Saul, or David, or Jonathan, someone of stature."

"You're right, yet your name bothers me, no matter, another has had the same sometime. No, I haven't known you, you're fortunate to have encountered us, lone travelers are at great risk from marauding bands."

"I make out well enough, none bother me, God goes before me with his shield."

"Why you and not others?"

"He watches over the old, the ugly, and the helpless."

"Ho, you have wit, old woman, you will flavor our conversations with your salt of the mind."

"Thank you, great sir; you could be David."

These men who would join David's band treated me well, possibly because they saw nothing of interest in the dirty hag I am. I did nothing to change their opinions. My claim to being God's spokesperson had little influence on the spice of their language, except to elicit a bawdy story from time to time, evidently meant as much for my ears as their own. Something about the magic of the sexes brings out lewd language occasionally, even with one no longer able to spark personal interest – almost as though they honor the memory of what has been, or might have been.

You think it an unlikely story that one who has attracted David could travel with men still in their potent years and go undetected? Need I explain that a dirty old woman holds no interest to a virile man? It is odd – the separation of physical care and physical desire, I was ignored during those times, even though not far removed from their presence. They had no reason to doubt my story, nothing to arouse suspicion.

Before I departed Palti, I experimented with skin dyes until I looked as old as needed and let my hair become matted. Palti winced each time he glanced at me, obviously, his mind has slipped, or he would have put me in bonds.

Do I protest too much, about being left alone? If you think so, you do not know men who are released from the restraints of convention, and why would I lie to you now?

An unprotected woman is fair game for a good many of them, as any woman knows who's found herself in the path of conquering armies, or simply at their mercy as servant or slave.

It is a rare man who refrains from partaking the fruit of conquered land when he's hungry. How long does it take a man to be hungry? Not long, and the hunger becomes ravenous.

Oh, you still think I am overstating for effect? Would a father give his daughter away for personal gain? That is slavery or forced prostitution and no man would do that to his own blood? Not related to the foregoing thought? Yes, it is; I've been there, surely you remember who did that. Where have you been during the telling of this tale? Selling daughters is the common practice, and not limited to kings.

Fathers want sons to carry on the line; they want daughters who'll attract a healthy marriage gift. Oh, yes, they pamper them when infants, when ripe and attractive to men, they become pawns in kings' maneuvers – for ordinary men, it is part of their struggle for survival.

For the shopper, they become plums for the choosing, with payment in coin, which surely passes through the mind, leaving taint along the way, little noticed by the buyer – or seller.

Who notices? The taint is on the one sold and bought – the female, the one with no say in the matter, when small, a girl is her papa's doll; when grown, she is his profit maker; at the basic level his means of survival. Oh, yes, sometimes with reluctance because of hearth memories, but sacrificed, nevertheless.

These things are the other half of the same story; the other half of men's understanding of women among them – those fashioned as Adam's companion. My head hurts.

I'm sorry if you are offended; I feel used by my father – though not abused by him physically; Papa was above reproach in that. In that, at least, Merab and I were fortunate. In the end, both of us were given away as punishment, not so different from being sold, or, were we sold? No coins passed, are lives less important?

With David, my bride price doesn't appear to be the same, but it was. The main difference being that I wanted the buyer to make the purchase. With Palti, it occurs to me, I don't know the price, if any. My cost was the loss of my pride, added to the agony of losing David.

Yes, the king is my father, I love him and hate him. I could attribute his actions to madness: treating us as pawns, as objects to be moved without thought to our wishes, are all men mad? Certainly not, they merely conform to customs and manners.

I know few who have shown no such selfish interest; those I do not love. Are women also mad that they are attracted to those who treat them as objects?

My traveling friends and I moved toward David's sanctuary in the land of Philistines, careful always for out-moving scouts of the constantly searching armies.

An incident occurred as I went into the dusk for personal care before sleep one evening: one from a wandering band slipped up and grasped around me from behind. I cried out, bit hard into his arm until my new friends, drawn by the scuffle, came running to drag him to the campfire.

When he saw the hag he'd attacked, dismay filled his face, I don't know if he even knew it was a woman he reached for in the darkness. Possibly he did, otherwise a knife might have ended my search.

My companions laughed with derision as he skulked away, adequately punished by humiliation. The evening became raucous with lewd suggestions, fortunately eased by their liking for their female comrade, the dirty old one.

AN UNBELIEVABLE THING

And then another shock, Palti has found me again, that after he vowed not to follow me.

"You disappoint me, Palti, why have you come after me?"

"You are needed at home to care for your sons."

"I have no sons at home, God has not trusted me with children."

"God has trusted you with five sons; it is your duty to return to give them the care of a mother."

"Stop playing games, you've lost your mind, what is this wild tale you tell?"

"Merab has fallen to sickness, and Adriel has brought them to you. She clearly said you were to have them, since they are of the same line though not your own birthing."

"Am I never to talk to David?"

"Who am I to say? I didn't bring the children; it was your sister who bore them, and her husband who delivered them to you on her direction. You wanted children, now you have five, it is well you're not small, little one."

"I didn't bargain for five, my whole life is changed."

"Then you will return?"

"I have no choice, they are mine since Merab is gone, I must not betray her trust again. Wait while I tell my companions; they'll not believe the old hag is not an old hag."

"Nor would I, had I not seen you when you departed our hearth. You are worse than when I last saw you, almost, I would leave you here, except for our sons, I would."

"God has dealt a hard blow to keep me from seeing David. Let us return to my boys."

"Yes, our lives have changed, who knows how we'll end, the fates have winding paths."

"Have you no belief in God, Palti?"

"The God drawn by the prophets is not friendly to me, what is he to you?"

"I'm still working on that, my friend, the God papa and David serve is not quite the same. David tells beautiful pictures of God between his plundering, killing expeditions, I am trying to sort the God from the David."

"*Your friendship has been long in coming.*"

"Need a man and wife be friends? I didn't know that was in the bargain, when papa gave me to you, did you ask if I would be your friend?"

"What would have been your answer?"

"It is a strange world we serve, Palti."

"There you've said it, we serve the world while trying to mix in a bit of God to alter the path unfolding before us."

"It sounds selfish, and probably is."

"Taking on five we've never seen is not selfish, it will help you forget David."

"I have forgotten him."

"Of course you have, that's why you continually chase though never quite catch him. That's why you ignore me in the midst of what should be love."

"What?"

"As Saul said, *I am 'not insensitive.'*"

"I'm sorry, Palti…. let's go to our children. I'm amazed, God has trusted me at last."

FIVE BOYS, AND DAVID

Can you imagine the jolt of assuming care of five boys you've never seen, and equally, who have never seen you?

We should turn them over to servants? You mistake our position, we are not wealthy, though I have some help. Papa could have given me to one of lower station, I owe him something for that.

Quickly family activities become routine, no, not routine. A family with five boys is never routine, tumult replaces routine and becomes routine. I'd forgotten what it's like to be in a household with boys, in this case not surrounded by servants, this time with no girls to dilute the uproar. Chaos reigns constantly, quiet is so unusual as to seem strange, it is to wonder what has gone wrong this time.

Work is increased three-fold; pressures, ten-fold. Palti's needs continue and must be accommodated; I am his wife. And I wanted children, I didn't say five; though for many mothers that is a small family, very small, they have no time for wandering thoughts other than sighing ... or crying when one is lost. Too often it comes to that.

Stories of David are never routine, therefore we shall continue, *now through the eyes of a mother of children not his, David's – fathered by another and born to the first who was given to him and passed now to the second, the one he paid for and accepted, the one who bore him no child, no son ... oh, oh, strange, but instantly they are part of the family ... not part of, they are the family!*

It has come out again, that undercurrent of thought turned toward David. I would never say that to Palti, it would distress him the more. As you saw, he is not insensitive, though you might mistakenly think so from my reporting, there is no need to make it worse for him.

Previously we spoke of David as he carried on his raids while in sanctuary with the Philistines ... during this time, he led a band of outlaws, not yet an army; each raid became a training mission for his motley band, each mission saw them more skilled at marauding and slaughter, apparently work they took to readily. Why would they not become better with practice? David is known for his ability to lead, which includes training for that activity, now with swords and spears at which he is as skilled as with the sling.

David suffers no great hardships, with two beautiful wives vying for his attention. It is unlikely they and others ignore David in the midst of their busy lives, each scrambling for his attention.

That haven began to unravel when Achish called David and his army to fight with them against the Israelites.

It is so innocent-sounding, the usual activity for David and his men except for who they were going out against: *David's own people*. Finally, David is in a trap that will end his hope of being king of Israel. When word goes out that David has joined the Philistines against his own, he will be through, his anointing for kingship wasted.

The great lad who killed Goliath will now have killed himself, he might as well cut off his own head and hand it to Saul that the Israelites might put it on a stake to spit upon, for that is what will happen. And I said David was not feeble-minded?

David took his men and walked among the Philistines. Immediately when the Philistine commanders saw David, they complained, "What are the Hebrews doing here?"

Was David simple? Or was he fully expecting what the commanders would say when they saw him, an enemy among them – a poison burr under the pack of the burro, and the journey just beginning?

If he could foresee and plan such subtle strategy, he was a man without equal as a leader of nations. At the very least, he is unusual.

I cannot know these things since I never thought to ask him, so I speculate.

As Achish said to his commanders of the Philistines, "Is not this David ... who has been with me now for days and years, and since he deserted to me, I have found no fault in him to this day." Did you hear the word '*years*'? Surely, longer than David would have liked.

Probably according to David's plan and to his relief, he and his ragtag army were sent home because of the protests, *the disaster to his future in Israel was avoided.* Was David simple or subtle, what would he have done had they not protested? We don't know.

We return with David and his army to their sanctuary at Ziklag.

Here they found that while they were with the army of Achish, the Amal'ekites had raided and burned the town, *carrying away all those in it, including David's beloved wives Ahin'o-am and Ab'igail.* "and David was greatly distressed; for the people spoke of stoning him, because all the people were bitter in soul, each for his sons and daughters. But David strengthened himself in the Lord his God."

Has David lost his halo? As you see, there were sons and daughters as I told you, as well as wives that were carried off, David did not foresee or take precautions for a surprise invasion.

After consulting the ephod to get instruction from God, David followed them with his six hundred. (*You see, also, I am unprejudiced in reporting.*)

So furious was the pursuit that two hundred of the six hundred fell out from fatigue.

When David finished slaughtering, only four hundred of the raiders escaped to return to their homes – this was not one of David's generous moments. I said *escaped*, not *released*. *His precious wives and all with them were brought back safe with the army.* In gratitude, David rewarded even the two hundred who fell out from fatigue, he was grateful indeed.

His sanctuary was over, once more David was on the run with his retinue, what skill it took to provide for them, to run with them. Not until later did I learn how difficult that was, much later from personal involvement. Stories at the time did not give details, except those that polished the halo of the motley contingent, by this time, David could have had as many recruits as he wished.

We turn again to papa. According to reports, *papa* – no longer the brave leader with access to God – *consulted a medium at Endor* to hear what plans God had for him in this defense against the Philistines, which turned out to be his last. *In this battle I lost my brother-friend and two other brothers, four family members in all. Four family members gone and no one came to tell me.*

Word came as it did to the rest of Israel, first as an unbelievable rumor, soon unrefutable fact, cold gloom, then relief that the inevitable had happened, then fear of the unknown, yet not, for

MICHAL'

David is waiting ... not for me.

When papa saw his sons gone, his commanders, and all the men with them, he fell on his own sword. He was old, it was time.

This was the end of the Saul era, and my dreams are gone, what do I mean? Do you not know it is too late for me? Fate has passed me by.

I now have lost my sister, three brothers, and my papa – and two other women claim my husband. I have Palti and five sons we are bringing up for my sister, *the world is askew.*

The David Kingdom so long in the making has begun.

We may speculate, but we'll never know what would have happened had the Philistines not rejected David and his small army before the battle against Israel. Many things might be different. You have a good imagination, I will not try to list them for you.

Saul reigned many years, at first he wanted to be a good king. As time went on, his mind played tricks on him, and hence on his people.

God must have loved him in the beginning; in the end, Saul no longer pleased God, and he would not answer when Saul called. In desperation, papa turned to mediums, in the realm of witches. You heard, he was desperate, normal channels to God were no longer open to him.

Did we finish the story of papa consulting the medium at Endor? It doesn't seem so important now, papa is gone ... *yes, I cried for him, never will there be another like him.*

CHAPTER XII
DAVID, KING OF JUDAH,
only one tribe followed him.
War, Women, Worship, and Repentance

David's mind has not gone bad; there have been no sudden dementia changes in his actions, he has always had an eye for women, though for a time I absorbed that interest.

That does not mean his interests are unchanged, they've not shifted to other things; rather, they have intensified with other women, I have watched this happen, mostly from a distance.

Now we pick up his story again. His story is my story, and Palti's, much as Palti would have it otherwise.

When on the third day after the battle David heard of the death of Saul, *he ordered the one who brought the news slaughtered. Did you hear that? Shall I repeat it?*

The story is a long one, but sufficient to say, David justified the killing because the messenger claimed to have finished off Saul since he knew he couldn't live. Though he hadn't finished Saul – it was intended as a self-serving boast – it was enough for David.

And David lamented over Saul his enemy and Jonathan his friend. In a way, papa was his friend, too.

Then the Lord sent David to Hebron, where the men came up and anointed him king over Judah, which he ruled for seven years and six months.

It is here that we come to my surviving brother Ish-Bosheth's burst of ambition. Always he's had secret corners not easy to understand; drawing off by himself, the quick mind, the only one not accepting Jonathan's appointment as first son. Ishvi and I had much in common, except the important thing, he was male. I swear to you,

MICHAL'

I am content being a woman; it has its rewards. But let's not go into that again.

Abner the son of Ner at once saw the potential in Ishvi so long overlooked behind Jonathan's bold leadership. "I can make you a great king, greater than your father; we can be a team."

"What of David? He is not yet a victim of war."

"Well, what of David, has he become king all these years when his supporters tried to back him? I don't believe he wants to be king, you are a beautiful man, Ishvi, the only surviving son of Saul, tall as your father, greater than David, beside you, he looks like a decorated strutting pigeon. The Israelites will follow you, forget David."

"You're right, Abner, he doesn't want to be king, else why has he waited while papa piddled away the kingdom. He is an indecisive weakling; you have my permission. Yes, we'll grow old together leading Israel to her glory."

"Long did I suspect that Jonathan had no interest in Saul's kingdom; though little did I dream you, *already approaching forty*, would be the one to follow him."

"I am not old, Abner; no woman has accused me of that."

"Oh no, there's no doubt of your vigor in that department, in that you are like your father."

Abner was as good as his word, almost, only the tribe of Judah rejected him in favor of David. All the rest went with Ishvi and Abner.

Yes, one tribe only followed David to begin his nascent kingdom.

For two years, then, Ishvi's dream tried to flower while he played at being king, warring, killing, and fathering – the duties of kings.

At the pool of Gibeon, it came to an end when twelve servants of Ishvi met twelve servants of David and were split by their swords. Abner with his survivors ran before the servants of David, Saul's great general, now Ishvi's, so soon running again. Abner should have known better than to fall into a trap set by the master of traps, the master of boy against giant. The years of chasing David misled him, dulled his memory, caused him to believe David a witless coward.

For David, some of these years of divided tribes was involved in warring with other parts of Saul's former kingdom – while they also warred among themselves; Ishvi's control under Abner lasted briefly before disintegration began.

Was my listing of Abner over Ishvi's leadership a mistake? It well describes the situation, if we remember that Ishvi always wanted to lead but had no practice and possibly no aptitude.

Ishvi and David were alike in some ways, with a major difference: David mounted the wind and clung tightly to the mane through the wildest storms. His mount was solidly conditioned, more often attacking, but, when necessary, running, as from papa and Abner, sometimes from others.

In another way, too, they were different: Ishvi went to God out of habit, David often in penitence, trusting even when unclean.

Most facts of record need no great elaboration from me, we pass over them quickly. Some are as well known but muted, glossed over because of David's reputation grown from his beautiful words.

No one before has used words as beautifully as David, he turns my stomach with his worship poetry while he entertains women who have his attention for a time.

You imagined I must not know about the others, of course I know, how could I not?

We have covered his marriages to Ab'igail and Ahin'o-am, that needs not repeating. One would think two women would satisfy his cravings, apparently they did not, for stories continued to circulate of other beautiful women who caught his attention, these got as much attention as stories of his wars; he was equally successful at both.

It is no wonder, the women, that is, because he is a beautiful man and he is king ... I am surprised that God allows David so much freedom in his excesses. David often told me about God's part in anointing him for kingship long before it came about.

I can see why God chose him; there is no doubt about his ability as a leader; on the other hand, God withdrew his favor to papa because of his excesses, why does David continue unchecked?

Are we going too fast for you? Let us review his behavior with females.

I was first, actually second choice – because he had no opportunity for me when he was offered Merab.

MICHAL'

When it came my turn, he was faithful to me for some time; it appeared it would continue, he said it always would be so. It did not continue; he has forgotten me, if David's pledge is of no value, whose is?

The affair with Ab'igail was next; a married woman that I am convinced he set out to entrap when he saw her beauty. Ab'igail's response outmatched his own scheme, neither she nor David could have predicted the drunken-sot husband's cooperation when he fell over dead for them.

David tells of God going before him in battle; I wonder if God went before him in his plan to get Ab'igail.

Of course David would make a better husband than did Nabal, because of that, did God assist David in his scheme? If so, what marriage is safe? I will not believe God did that. You do not agree that it was planned before he sent his soldiers to request provisions? You are very generous, then, to the beautiful man of words.

You do not think God assisted him, He did not assist, nevertheless allowed it and continued His blessing on David? Why? Do beautiful words impress God that much?

I doubt it, surely God is brighter than any of his creation ... even than David?

Am I blaspheming? If so, it is not intended, really I am questioning that David always was blessed as much by God as so many believe, maybe even as much as he believes.

Of course there is no doubt about his guilty conscience after each of his great episodes of sin, of his pleas for forgiveness, of his hunger for God's presence. Surely God blessed the seeking of forgiveness and hunger for his presence.

It is commitment to God's commandments, when sin in the form of beautiful women tempted him, that is in doubt. Never did he allow his conscience to deter his amorous activities.

Now I have broken my word to you: *that I would not bore you with details of his marriage to Ab'igail*. I get carried away with these ramblings.

Where were we?

No. 3, AHIN'O-AM, continued.

Now I recall, we were at the point of talking about his third wife, Ahin'o-am of Jezreel. There is no juicy tale about her, she caught David's eye, she was not yet married, he asked for and got her, why should he not, is he not king of Judah? Three wives are not uncommon. She is only one more in his harem, his stable of women. Is that being catty? You know the expression? Oh, yes, you and I have much in common.

Possibly he did not love her? Possibly not, but he slept with her and fathered children by her, no one required him to do that. The same is true of each of the other four he married before the end of his time as king of Judah. All of the six? Of course, he fulfilled his husbandly obligations to all of them.

I could wish he considered it dutiful obligation, it would be foolish wishful thinking. Later events confirm this speculation, is this too much revealing of my heart? Every woman alive has thoughts never expressed, wishes buried because of constrictive customs. Likely, if spread about, this revealing could hasten my end.

He had six wives who bore him a first son during that seven and one half year hiatus. But it isn't a gap, is it? Much more: it is when his roots go down into firm soil, setting up the great vine, a climbing rose? No, not that either. Ivy? Possibly, if seen in its most developed stage. If you've not seen massive ivy roots, you can't understand the comparison.

Daughters and second or third sons, or fourth, such as there were during this time, received no special notice. Children of concubines, none at all.

During these years, David paid particular attention to his decorum and public image; he yet hoped to gain a united kingdom. What, then, of his women? Beautiful hero David was indulged them by adoring subjects.

Finally, I have no hope of being recalled to my position of first wife in his household. Would I be first in the harem of king David? Who would want that? Not I after his public excesses with women. Our times of sharing would not be the same; that would not be possible when he shares with six others, God has not seen fit to bless women except as they are blest in pleasing men. Sadly, we

MICHAL'

accommodate them with little consideration in return.

David recognizes the role of women and makes the most of it. That leads to this question, Why would he want me back now? What would I do if he were to recall me?

That is a foolish thought – only one response is possible.

He has been stable for some time now – possibly he is settling down in his domestic life, if not with his warring, after all, why would any man want more than six wives? Oh, yes, and concubines, they, too, are women and share the role. (Don't twist your face, you are not the one involved ... tell me if I go too far.)

It may be that God finally has warned him, threatened to do to him as was done to papa Saul when his excesses went on and on.

Our five sons occupy my hours, few remain to worry about David's doings. I must turn my thoughts to other things; nothing is gained by dwelling on what was, and will not be again.

I can see why God is tender toward David when he pens those songs of integrity, love, loyalty to God, his cry for attention from the Lord, for forgiveness. (Already I've broken my resolve not to dwell on David's doings.)

Every noble thought in that active mind is molded into beautiful form to be seen by God and man, I am moved by his words; all Judah and Israel have tasted and found them good. It is the excesses so much resembling papa's that worry my heart ... returning to him immediately after promising new thoughts.

When these words of David became known, I saw papa again, *"Morning by morning I will destroy all the wicked in the land, cutting off all the evildoers from the city of the Lord."* Yet with so much beauty, who can worry long about holy words wrapped in intent to slaughter? Were it not for knowledge of his works in war, I would attribute them to poetic expression. What is that he calls *evildoers, those who are not of his household, his faith?*

David is tasting the power of power. He is beautiful and a brilliant leader. *Men and women will follow him wherever he leads, he is no longer a simple shepherd boy. Where will it be?*

I must believe God has chosen well. Because God's hand is on him, does that mean his excesses are approved, that his poetic flow covers all it overshadows? Suddenly I tremble after words of treachery. And then I remember, that was long ago, not today.
It is over, what was to be, is.

Seven and one half years as king of Judah. During that period, the house of Saul gradually came apart through warring between themselves, the final breakup and turn toward David involved papa's former concubine, Rizpah – without her part, it likely would not have been.

And a shattering development that changed my life again. The story is not long, I will tell it, or re-tell, though some of it will await later telling.

Abner, the son of papa's General Ner, is a name we knew well, for years he has been in a place of command. After the death of Saul and his commanders, Abner survived in the upper circle of manipulating commanders. It was he who manipulated Ishvi into control over the greater part of Israel, with increased power came women.

Later, Abner went to concubine Rizpah after papa was out of the way, this angered my brother Ishvi, who challenged Abner,

"*Why have you gone in to my father's concubine?*"

With so much flouting of sex customs, Abner likely didn't expect the challenge. In his instant anger, the desire for revenge against Ishvi possessed him, even if it meant helping *David, the one who eluded him so long,* it made the opening David had been awaiting.

Angry Abner came to him with an offer to bring over all Israel to again combine the kingdom under one leader. Done out of a poor motive, but exactly what David wanted. Leaders rarely look at or question motives in such cases; ends justify motives as well as means.

THE IMPOSSIBLE HAPPENED TO ME

It was then the impossible happened, *David demanded my return to him before he would accept the united kingdom.*

What a demand! All these years and not a word from him, all the other women between, now he wants me back. Why would he do that? I was not consulted any more than when I was given to Palti, or for that matter, when I went to David the first time.

Without warning, soldiers came with orders to take me to David. My boys cried, as did Palti, as did I. We have been together several years now, we have a family; a family may not be torn apart without pain – anguishing pain; our tears were ignored. You thought this was my greatest wish? How we confuse life, and our friends, for a fact, we confuse ourselves!

I did not kick and scream as they escorted me away.

But Palti did, at least he cried and pleaded with them; he followed until Abner ordered him to return home to care for his boys. Merab's boys, my boys, finally Palti's boys alone to raise. Palti has now been thrice blessed by Saul's act when he gave me to him: a wife who loves another – her husband; now five boys, grandsons of the man who started all this; and a third blessing, the wife he has come to love against all reason, torn from his home.

Would he undo it all and start over if he could? I will never know; we were given no time for good-bye's. If his reaction is a true drawing of his wishes, his agony, then I do know … Palti is mine without a doubt.

Our lives are a jumble beyond belief.

Along the way the soldiers repeated David's words many times, *"Good, I will make a covenant with you; that is, you shall not see my face, unless you first bring Michal', Saul's daughter, when you come to see my face."*

He sent to my brother Ishvi with these words, *"Give me my wife Michal', whom I betrothed at the price of a hundred Philistine foreskins."* Actually, two hundred in the bulging sack, long ago dog food, well he knew. The men laughed about that, including the suggestion of dog food, as though it were a joke; recognizing my poor place in annals of the kingdom.

That is interesting, Papa set the price at a hundred men's lives; David doubled it, as though they were trinkets, astounding everyone, now again the lives of others mean nothing to him where his desires are concerned. Once more my life is involved, but how differently

– returning now to a home occupied by six other wives. *Oh, God of my people, what have you done to us, to Palti, our boys, to me. I said I would never do this, and I am doing it,* no choice was given me.

What is it about foreskins? Is it because the Israelites are separated from that symbol of manhood very young, is nothing else important? Is it only papa and David who are fixated with sex, or all men, or all people? Or am I picking at nits, have I changed, was I once so obsessed? How have we come to such a pass? In olden times was it so?

War, sex, religion, food and shelter, what else is there? The listing is pretty much in order, not even sex will deter men from war, though they never miss a chance to profit in that way at the winding down of carnage, possibly it is tension relief.

Or, as I asked papa, is it a bait used to entice men into risking their lives? More than ever, I believe it is so, when it is over, they worship, or ask forgiveness if they have emotional need of cleansing. David is drawing a pattern.

I saw you flinch then, obviously you have yet to accept that this is truth, very well, you may soon go to the records to determine the truth. *Remember, I make no claim for my opinions; they are not included as truth.*

In these opinions, you must notice my disagreement with the too often disregard of the Commandments. Of course, I'm a woman complaining of personal treatment, of my husband's disregard of God's laws, in this instance affecting my whole life. You don't see the connection? You believe I twist the Law to show my own plight? Is Palti my husband, or is it David?

David expresses such beauty in his words, God sounds so close when he says them. Is there no reality in religion? Will it always be so? Surely the word of God finds lodging somewhere.

Earlier, I compared David's excesses with those of Saul and wondered if sometime he would surpass papa in them, already he has passed him in some and continues unabated. *In other ways they are so different, papa lacked David's worship side and appreciation of beauty.*

I am David's wife again, and he comes to me, sometimes, but now, I am not alone, sharing David is not my choice to make. Seven wives share his favors, and others called concubines, he whispers the same words in my ear; they have not the same meaning. What have I done to myself, or did God know what was in store for me, was it, is it, God's will?

While David makes love, I think of Palti and five boys. Did I say love, is that love? (Vaguely, I remember a similar thought in another setting.)

Once papa and I had a conversation about camp prostitutes and who uses them; I wondered why the women are there, what they think about as they work, what life means to them, how different or similar they are to others of us ... now I understand a little better. Where are the using men in the scale of values? Do they pen beautiful phrases of worship before or after? Or are they clods, some dirt, infested with worms? Can God love them between, or in spite of their personal lives? I suppose it depends on repentance in sacrifices, surely God knows the heart.

Once upon a time, no, for a long time, I longed to return to David, almost on any terms. Now I am here and question why he called me back. He has no need of me, I am as one in his flock except that I bear him no lamb, possibly the only one who has failed him in that which is so important to men – yes, and to women, too.

He uses me as a link to the throne through his marriage with Saul's daughter – as though he needs it. If a male child were from our union it would be even better in his eyes, I've given up hope of that. Now I say, *he uses me*.

If he knew my mind, he'd kill me. No, he would have someone else do it, then he would write a psalm, and people would call him wonderful.

To some extent, he again turns to me as one who can hear his thoughts without repeating them. In that, possibly, I do him an honest service, involved with, but separated from the act involved. Did I speak correctly? Yes, until now, none other has heard these musings.

Much of what you hear is public information, had his private comments or my thoughts been repeated, I would not be here to speak with you. His sons could do him great damage and survive, not so his wives.

ABNER'S PLOTTING PAYS RICHLY

The crowning achievement of David's long sojourn came when Abner's plotting helped bring all Israel to join with Judah in the kingdom under David. It came so easily when the grapes were ripe. How Ishvi was persuaded to cooperate, I do not know, at that stage, possibly he was afraid to oppose David.

A sentence or two of superlatives could end the tale here, from that time everything increased, including David's fame and excesses. How they took place and who was touched by the events is another chapter in David's chronicles. Now we turn that page in his life.

CHAPTER XIII
DAVID, KING OF ALL ISRAEL, AIDED BY RIZPAH,
Saul's former concubine (Then the impossible happened)

Abner's help in making David king of all Israel cost him his life soon afterward. Many have found it so over the years – being involved with David, that is, even with my disasters, I was among the fortunate. How few lives are what early dreams say they will be.

Being in camp with Abner made him available to Jo'ab, David's nephew ... whose brother Abner had killed in battle. *Jo'ab evened the score by murdering Abner*, a not uncommon activity these days. One killing begets another, killing goes on and on, justified by pointing to God.

Many scores remained to be settled from the years of warring among the tribes before they united under David; others were added under David; they, too, awaited settling.

Killing is a way of life for our men. It is amazing that anyone remains alive, victors slaughter male, female, old, and young alike. Life is no more important than my bride's price, one hundred, two hundred, what is the difference? A foreskin trinket, a man murdered, no, two hundred, to get a woman, this woman, later cast aside, possibly to teach her a lesson.

Once, to me, war was a word meaning excitement, victory, glory, when papa talked of his victories my flesh tingled.

When David talked to God about his plans and beautiful dreams, I was proud.

I lived with Palti, who is a man of peace, I raised five boys – my boys ... *my values have changed, war and killing frighten me.*

Again David talks of victories, the glorious word of heroes. I see blood, bodies, dying boys who cry for water, for help; babies run through with a sword because they are children of losers in tribal games.

Stories of raids and booty raise specters, women forced by men, women like myself, younger women, girl children eight or ten years old, girls still babies in emotions, suddenly moved from babyhood to the pain of age, finding despair, useless rage. Rage is a waste of time and emotion at the final end of such a session. What is proper, useful, then? Nothing at all, calling on God doesn't work, but we do it anyway, yet God is our only hope, possibly in death. Yes, I call upon God in anguish, my ravishing is semi-with-my unwilling consent.

The glories of war have vanished in my heart. War glory is a fantasy bubble, but for our nation, for David, it goes on and on – the duty and honor of men; apparently, one of the duties and burdens of women, also. Possibly we should accept the physical and emotional damage with the same enthusiasm with which men face war; though I wonder if all of them go forth with joy.

There must be the same spark of humanity in them, awaiting the breath of God to touch it into flame. Is there no way for God to speak his love side to us? From David comes word that God leads him, tells him what to do, how to war, to continue killing, David believes what he says, and it may be true.

God has not spoken to me; who am I to say what God tells David? He is the one who speaks with God. Does God love only David and those who follow him? Is David hearing well?

I want to hear about a God who loves children, who tells no one to hurt and kill them; one who reaches out to losers as well as winners in war. Papa said I have no bent toward religion, he may have been right in that. Is it wrong to want a gentle God?

This is burdening my spirit; I must move to other thoughts.

I will speak more about David's love life after he called me back, this time to a harem. That may not be beautiful, but it's not depressing now that I've accepted my lot. Yet, in a way, it is depressing, for he carried his passions to new heights, more breaking of Commandments. You will hear about that shortly.

MICHAL'

You thought it would please me to return to David? I led you to believe that throughout this telling? It would have if neither he nor I had changed, let me tell you of an incident, hear my words carefully; they are true. The slant he gives to his actions does not tie with what you and I know of his activities.

"*As the ark of the Lord came into the city of David, (I) Michal' ... looked out of the window, and saw King David leaping and dancing before the Lord; and (I) ... despised him in (my) heart.*" As so often happens in religious fervor, he went naked in public as an expression to God ... such is blessed by God?

You may chastise me for impertinence to the king, or for arrogance, or you may call it jealousy, whatever you call it, I could not hold my tongue when he returned to the household.

Like a shrew I spoke to him, "*How the king of Israel honored himself today, uncovering himself today before the eyes of his servants' maids, as one of the vulgar fellows shamelessly uncovers himself.*"

Uncovered himself? That is not the impression you had of this episode? *Examine the record; it is true*; he did not deny it.

There was no apology in him, brazenness, arrogance showed in his words – all attributed to God; from his words I knew trouble was ahead. "*I will make merry before the Lord. I will make myself yet more contemptible than this, and I will be abased in your eyes; but by the maids of whom you have spoken, by them I shall be held in high honor.*"

This is not the David who played and sang for King Saul, the boy I loved. I had heard stories of such activity, but not before had I seen David so debase himself, he tries to make his public depravity appear to be holy work for God. Some believe him, it is so sad!

He did not send me back to Palti ... it would have been better if he had. That was the end of what remained of our relationship.

Still I had hoped that by a miracle a child would be born to me, even from David. It was not to be, *from that day he did not come to me.*

Much of what you hear from that time on was not gained directly from David to me, but through the ears and tongues of others. There is now no reason to shield him, you may as well know the infamous story that prepared the next king.

First let me say, *"And David took more concubines and wives from Jerusalem, after he came from Hebron; and more sons and daughters were born to David."* Among those born to him was one called Solomon, the greatest of his sons. Surely, you've heard of him?

My jealousies were not contrived from the wind. You've heard the increasing extravagances of his passions. By this time, David imagined he, the king, had approval for blessing the world with his offspring, basically that means his lust for female beauty could be satisfied without restraint. To a large degree it was.

The story goes this way, one afternoon while walking on his roof, David looked over and saw a beautiful woman bathing.

Why she was bathing in a place clearly visible from David's favorite privacy walk we may guess. David's appreciation of beauty was well known, it may be assumed she knew her own physical attraction, *'may be assumed?'*

Would you give him charity and say he did not know she was married? *He did know,* in fact when he asked about her, one of his men said, *"Is not this Bathshe'ba, the daughter of Eli'am, the wife of Uri'ah the Hittite?"*

That should have ended the story, of course it did not. Possibly he considered her more beautiful than all others, in any case, he abandoned caution. *"So David sent messengers and took her; and she came to him, and he lay with her. Then she returned to her house. And the woman conceived; and she sent and told David, 'I am with child.'"*

How easily it happens for some, and, yes, long ago it was clear, it was I, not David, who was barren. God overlooked me when the child producing function was considered. Had David known that, would he have called me? Knowing him as I do, my guess is: Yes, he called me back after the long separation, knowing full well, *and it wasn't all a political decision.*

David's following actions are seen as in clear water, at first his intent was to hide his guilt from her husband, Uriah. David sent for Uriah and, after small talk, told him to go home and sleep a night with his wife. *That failed because of Uriah's loyalty to his fellow soldiers,* he could not take his pleasure while they slept on the battle field....

Once more David tried to lure him by eating with him and making him drunk, hoping to deaden his ideals of loyalty to his fellow warriors. Again the plot of David failed, once more Uriah would not sleep with his wife.

It causes one to wonder if, by some intuition, Uriah knew what had gone on in his absence. Or that he knew his wife so well, he knew it would happen when he was away.

At this point the ill use of power reached its zenith, David sent a note to commander Jo'ab at the battle site, *"Set Uri'ah in the forefront of the hardest fighting, and then draw back from him, that he may be struck down, and die."*

With this, David succeeded in releasing Bathshe'ba from her marriage pact. Pure, holy, haloed David acting out his heart, *the worst part of it. That battle was set up so that several soldiers would die, in order that Uriah would die, in order that David could have another woman of his choice.*

Once more the innocent die because of David, this time without doubt, planned deliberately for lust of another man's wife; this is a matter of record.

Does this further confirm earlier suspicions of plots to steal women from husbands?

It is the man who was my husband I am speaking about, my heart is heavy, our marriage is over, but he will not release me to my family, my Palti, my boys.

David has never tried to put a God face on the Bathshe'ba episode, although in many other instances of his women, he said God gave them to him. In this of Bathshe'ba, he was consumed with lust and would have the woman at any price, even defying a Command of God ... abetted by his officers, tolerated, excused by his people.

After Bathshe'ba's mourning period, David brought her to his house and she was his wife....

The Lord was not pleased about this and the son she bore from their early joining did not live, though David, as was his custom, fasted and prayed for the child.

When the child died, David went into the temple and worshipped, but did not put her aside. Evidence follows, it is so.

BATHSHE'BA BIRTHS SOLOMON

Bathshe'ba continued to be his wife, and he slept with her. *Again she bore him a son who was Solomon, later to be the king who was known for his wisdom, and his women.* It is said, the Lord loved him, the Lord is more forgiving than I.

It is difficult to be objective about this when so many of us in the household are affected.

Running the household is complicated unnecessarily when David reverts to his youth, as though the years and his wives and concubines did not happen. Reverts? How can one revert when it has been increasingly so?

At last David and I are on speaking terms again, after his disgraceful public display, it was easy to hold him responsible for our differences.

For some time I was isolated simply because he ignored me as though I were not there. Again I became a non-person in the household, soon that wore thin, almost anything would have been better. Doing nothing is the worst of assignments – standing at a turn in the trail holding a directional flag would be better. I might even have welcomed serving his needs occasionally had I thought he would want me, but I was afraid to approach him.

With nothing better to do, I was soon involving myself in ordering the household – without authority to do so. I have told you of the several intelligent women around David, around each other and me. All with ambition, each saw herself as the natural choice for leader of the flock.

The household became a nesting place for arguments and bedlam, at times the household more resembled a den of jealous hyenas than the dwelling of civilized human beings, more than that, God's chosen beings.

Having been out of the circle, my position as first wife had been ignored too long to happen again instantly. Sometimes, though, skills I had learned from mama lubricated the friction. My inclination was to turn my back on their stabbing word attacks, but I could not for long.

You might think David's qualities of leadership would work as well in the household as with armies, not so, jealous wives are slightly different than ambitious generals…. *You knew that?*

David has a keen eye for beauty, fortunately he also has skills in leadership.

When he finally called me into his private presence I expected once more to be drawn into his harem activities, with pounding heart I awaited his words. (*I am ashamed.*)

"I have watched your skill in ordering the household, Michal', since you have no children to care for, no other gainful activity, you may as well put order into this den of hyenas."

"That is why you called me?"

"Did you have something else in mind, my dear?"

"No, David, that is behind us."

"Possibly behind you, not behind me, I am yet young."

"I will care for your harem, not for your physical needs. You no longer need my attentions."

"You will care for any need I ask, Michal', have you forgotten that you are my wife?"

"No, David."

"You will come to my bed when I call."

"Yes, I will come when you call, must I accept with joy?"

"I have no need of a woman who does not please me. With your spirit, I should return you to Palti, no, that might please you. Besides, now that I have accepted you again in these walls, you may as well serve a purpose."

With that, David charged me with running the household and keeping order among the women. It seems so natural that it didn't occur to me to mention it earlier. My experience under mama's training was time well spent, she must have sensed our need, though we didn't see the importance then.

Finally, I better understand mama, she was not the prosaic person I thought her to be. Directing a household can fill hours and give purpose to life.

Have you imagined yourself a wife in a harem, or possibly as a concubine? This even has allowed me to understand the mind of women caught in unfortunate circumstances, we do what we must. Have I said that before?

The other side of the coin is not prettier when seen without the distortion of glory. The only real advantage of the ordinary man is his wider choice of a woman, or women, if that is his aim.

Why do I not say *Wife*? So few consider marriage morally binding; few are like Palti. I hope he has taken another wife to care for our boys, I do not have the courage to inquire.

STUPID, STUPID ... (The alternative is worse.)

David did some stupid things which upset the household and made my task more difficult, one of the worst was that he abetted incest between two of his offspring: his son Amnon with his half sister Tamar. Oh, surely, God did not sanction this.

A suspicion lurks in the deep of my mind that David may have abetted this sin in remembrance of his own somewhat similar misdeeds; though I prefer to think of it as stupidity instead of deliberate.

In a family as large as this with so many half brothers and sisters, it is as being part of a clan, incest sometimes happens, although seldom abetted by a parent. This is one better forgotten, but it is begun, so we will be brief.

Amnon apparently wanted Tamar so badly that he enlisted help of a cousin who suggested feigning illness and asking David to send Tamar to tend him.

Amnon's words to David were, *"Pray let my sister Tamar come and make a couple of cakes in my sight, that I may eat from her hand."* Who in his right mind would not suspect that, especially David? Apparently he did not, unless my earlier unwanted suspicion is true, he sent her without question.

She pleaded with Amnon, even suggested David might override custom and give her to him if he would wait. She did not object to being his woman, it was the manner she could not accept.

Amnon would not wait but took her by force, knowing she was a virgin. Immediately he hated her and sent her away, thus ruining the life of a beautiful woman.

Along with ruining the life of a woman, long lasting disaster came to my well functioning household. So quickly it happens, without warning, in the end it cost the life of Amnon, who was slain by beautiful Ab'salom – David's son, Tamar's brother – and put Ab'salom on the run for some time. The end was disaster for several.

Will you agree David made a stupid decision, if not evil? The flight of Ab'salom after he took vengeance left the household bereft of joy.

Oh yes, he had his own dwelling, it was there Tamar in desolation went to her self-imposed isolation after she was violated.

However, my responsibility spread to the larger family as they took their privacy. David's assignment of duties put me in a position of family power, not insignificant. In a strange way, my early ambitions were coming to bloom, limited by David's aging decisions.

I remonstrated with David when word came to me what had happened as a result of his strange granting of Amnon's lustful request, "What were you thinking, David, to allow that? Could you not see his purpose? You allow your sons too much leeway."

"Amnon made a mistake, but he was a good son; God forgives mistakes; you are jealous that you gave me no son."

"You are putting your own house and mine into disorder by such thinking."

"It is not your house, you are assigned to keep order in it, not to interfere with my judgments."

"And you are making it difficult by flaunting customs, even skirting the Commandments. A child could tell Amnon's intent; you would not have allowed that in your early years. Ab'salom your favorite son is gone; your beautiful daughter will not show her face out of her house, when will it end?"

"It will not end, life goes on, the attraction of man and woman will always be. Sometimes it causes trouble, but it is inevitable – God so designed it. Ab'salom will return when he has done penance for killing his brother; Tamar will come out when she is ready, I've talked to God about these things. You are a jealous woman; tend to your duties."

The last sounds strangely familiar ... only with David do I lose my temper now and he continues as he wishes, pays me no more attention than a discarded cloak. I get no help from him.

It was three years before David allowed Ab'salom to return, when he returned, he was kept away from the king two years additional. Once again David had made a serious mistake, this one even more serious in terms of the kingdom.

A worm grew in Ab'salom's heart toward his father, nourished by the adulation of the people – something David may have understood and feared; remembering the outcome in his own case with Saul.

Fed by people's adulation and his own resentment, Ab'salom set about to steal the hearts of the men of Israel from David. That conspiracy grew until a messenger came to David saying, *"The hearts of the men of Israel have gone after Ab'salom."*

DAVID FLEES, AS IN HIS YOUTH

At this, David gathered up all his household and fled, except ten concubines who were left to keep the house; he did not need them with him, how could he with so many others?

You thought it was sour grapes when I talked of his many concubines? Not so; exaggeration would be difficult. Ten were not missed.

And our company was in the hundreds, six hundred of the Gittites kept intact from his running years out of sentiment, besides those of the royal company and of the army faithful to David – many thousands.

What did they think? *David the conqueror fleeing again as in his youth!*

There is no way to know why David ran – if he had grown fearful in his later years, if he thought he had lost most of his following with the people, or if he wished not to kill his beautiful son. Killing has been a way of life for David, but he will not kill his sons – in that he was like papa. The other possibility is that he truly trusted God and had no word from him except to flee.

Now we give attention to Ab'salom, leader of the rebellion. He, too, found or created increasing trouble in his decayed relationship with his father David.

Meanwhile, on the advice of David's counselor who had gone over to Ab'salom, "*...they pitched a tent for Ab'salom on the roof; and Ab'salom went in to his father's concubines in the sight of all Israel.*" He chose to flaunt his father by taking the concubines David left behind – sin in the mode David had allowed Amnon, incestuous in principle if not actual, surely done deliberately as vengeance against David for the five years isolation.

Those were the ten concubines left behind by David to care for the house, how many of the ten were involved with Ab'salom, there is no way to say, possibly all of them.

This may have been the last time they knew a man, for when David returned, he did not go to them again, another instance of women suffering for the deeds of men – if that is suffering, being deprived of their attention. It, really, isn't a question, most would consider it suffering.

Also, it was another time when innocents suffered for David's actions, and now his son Ab'salom – beautiful Ab'salom, who, like his father could have any woman he wanted. Instead, he went to his father's concubines, the worst insult possible. Some time back, I compared the lot of men and women, without great advantage for either ... here Ab'salom was the sinner. The women victims suffered for his sin.

His trouble came from cankerous resentment and as a result of choosing the wrong counselor, one who traitorously sent word to David of the counsel he'd given, thus setting off David's wrath.

Of course David did not go to them again; why would he use women used by another? In this case, his son. Would that women could be as demanding, life would change, on the other hand, virginity was not necessary if the woman attracted him enough. Need we mention examples?

Possibly David is gaining some wisdom in that, often, he turns to the Lord for help. It's possible he always did this, though his excesses blinded me to his good points. I continue to wonder if he always hears what God says.

Now that I am *not* so emotionally involved with David, it is easier to see his strengths. Not as emotionally involved? A friend who knows me well says, "If you believe that, you will believe anything." I am as emotionally involved with David as ever, only in a different way.

Ab'salom and all the thousands of Israel's army set out after David and his thousands. Having missed the running years with David, not before have I been with a fleeing army. Thousands of fleeing people with their animals of burden and food supply make a great undulating, living, flowing, noisy, confused river on dry land. The dogs, chickens, sheep, oxen, asses, children, women, bearers, supplies, weapons, all go along unless they are expendable – old crippled, ornery.

Strangely, I am completely happy in this confusion; here my household is expanded to multitudes, David expects the same order as at home, not possible in the chaos he has caused; you will remember, when he granted Amnon's lascivious request – all this began there. Nevertheless, the women are moving with some degree of order, as much as can be expected in these conditions.

Where do women and children hide while the battle rages? I see no place to hide, history has not indicated that there was compassion for the innocent, it is no wonder they call on God for help.

Finally, David sent his thousands out to do war with his son's armies with these words, *"Deal gently for my sake with the young man Ab'salom."*

Ab'salom came out with his army to meet them, but David was counseled by his commanders not to join the battle. *Ab'salom died ... David lived.*

The events of Ab'salom's death is a household story, *"Ab'salom was riding upon his mule, and the mule went under the thick branches of a great oak, and his head caught fast in the oak, and he was left hanging between heaven and earth, while the mule that was under him went on."*

That did not kill him, but Joab did when he arrived with his armor-bearers, David's request for gentle dealing with his son was ignored in the heat of battle ... possibly, even, intentionally.

They did no more than David had done for years.

"O MY SON AB'SALOM"

When David received the news, he said the famous words, *"O my son Ab'salom, my son, my son Ab'salom! Would I had died instead of you, O Ab'salom, my son, my son."*

This is a man who loved his son enough to give up a kingdom rather than kill him.

O that he had loved me as much.

When David returned to Jerusalem, he went not to the ten concubines but put them under guard alone for the rest of their lives. I would say, God have mercy on him for his stupidity, for blaming them for that which they did not of their own choice. They were forced, used by a man; he has never been forgiving, in such, to those used against their will. David continues to do stupid things, possibly he thinks they should kill themselves because they are helpless to do anything else.

At this point in his life, it is too late, his patterns are set. He hears what he wants to hear from God in relation to such matters, or makes his own decisions. He had no need of the ten, they were few among many, they had little except his occasional attention when in his favor.

After being violated by his son, they got punishment for what they did not do, for being captive hosts (hostesses?). Where is justice, where is compassion for those caught in storms unsheltered?

One other thing I have kept from you from a long time earlier. It has bothered me so much that I will tell you and let you decide if it speaks of anything in particular or if it troubles only me.

Here it is: Early in the combined kingdom, when David attacked the Jeb'usites in Jerusalem through the water shaft, he is quoted as saying,

"'Whoever would smite the Jeb'usites, let him get up the water shaft to attack the lame and the blind, who are hated by David's soul.' Therefore it is said, 'The blind and the lame shall not come into the house.'" The Jeb'usites goaded him into that, but he put hate toward those who deserve mercy.

David is not known for persecuting the halt and the blind, *yet*, *clearly he set the storms of time against them with those words.* I would believe he let his anger twist his lips and speech.

He has proved himself human over and again, but that is a smallness he is not capable of. Whatever his motivation in that, God used his talents in other ways that will speak forever.

Since I have pledged candor and truth, *you may judge.*

SAUL'S EXCESSES LINGER, AND RETURN

These many years later, papa Saul's excesses have come back to hurt me.

Because of his actions I lost my five sons again. This is how it happened: For three years, a famine hung over Israel, starving her people. When David inquired of God why this thing was upon us, God told him it is because *Saul put the Gibeonites to death after Israel promised to spare them.*

To clear up the matter, King David asked the Gibeonites what they would have to satisfy the debt created by Saul. They ended the dispute by *asking for and getting seven of Saul's sons in exchange.*

They put to death his two sons by concubine Rizpah and five grandsons by his daughter Merab – Palti's and my sons. All my sons are dead; in the midst of young manhood, almost before they have lived, they are cut short before their time, my tear storage is empty as desert dried bone.

Is David's God without gentleness? Does David speak for him?

You have heard little about Rizpah, except that she was papa's second love that became first, and the daughter of Ai'ah. Actually you did not hear directly about the love, ordinarily, a concubine is not included as meriting official recognition, only wives have that privilege.

Mama knew Rizpah had taken her place with papa; I knew, everyone knew.

Who is Rizpah? She was Saul's concubine and the mother of two sons by him. That is all you would know except for the death of her sons; she loved her sons as any mother.

Oh, yes, one other of major importance: She was a key player in the move that brought Abner to David with the offer to bring all

Israel into David's kingdom. (Some saw her as beautiful even as she aged, I didn't.) Innocent, but key, nevertheless, she played a part in the joining of Israel under David. We've talked of it before.

When brother Ishbosheth challenged Abner for taking Rizpah after papa's death, Abner's resentment caused him to go to David with the offer.

David never thanked or credited Rizpah properly for her part in that. He may have remembered it with disfavor when granting her sons to death. (Review it, you may agree.)

She spread sackcloth and kept watch over their bodies from the beginning of harvest until the rains came, she fought off the carrion eaters and grieved. She was a woman who made the best of what she had and loved those she bore without honor.

Seven men – boys Rizpah and I had nourished – were hanged for papa's mistakes, mistakes from long ago. Seven more innocents paying for others' sins.

David gave them away for sacrifice without consulting me, without apology, without hesitation, without pain ... to himself.

Two mothers mourned.

God allowed me to be a mother through Merab, then took them away, I am looking for God through men who claim his presence. Mothers should be the ones who speak to God, then he might appear more gentle.

Have I forgotten Palti, who cared for our sons after I was taken away? I grieve with him for his loss, also; Palti, too, might seek a gentler God. What did I do? I can't speak of it, I am broken.

The Philistines warred with David again, except for his men, David would have died this time. They refused to let him go out at the next warring. *In earlier times, they could not have stopped him.*

Another battle and another 'Goliath' who was great of girth and *whose spear was like a weaver's beam* was slain by another youth.

And then one more war and another Goliath of great stature, *who had six fingers on each hand, and six toes on each foot, and a son of David's brother slew him.*

Long since had the brothers and their families joined in David's doings, except when they sought their own ends.

War goes on and on, over, and over, and over. The much warring is much killing, it leads to more begetting, whether with the camp followers, wives, or concubines, and women of the defeated. War is not conducive to holiness, moral purity.

Are you still of the opinion that abstinence prevails in the armies of Israel? Are men different when in war? Do they keep the Commandments about not killing? About another man's wife? About fornication?

Does David's life bear that out, did papa Saul's? Ab'salom's with papa's concubines, and all the rest? You did not think about women victims in war producing offspring? What of David with Uriah's wife, Bathshe'ba?

The child died, but it was born. David was not on the battlefield when that occurred; it was similar, but worse.

You don't think of her as a victim? In a sense she was, as was her husband, Uriah – though she used it to her advantage, certainly not to Uriah's.

Are not a man and woman involved? Somehow, God has ordained that when man and woman join, children follow, whether in marriage or not; *except for me and a few other unfortunates.*

Will their children be different? Will the mothers not love their babies?

Would you rather avoid this thought? Do you feel degraded by all this, and has the dwelling on wars and slaughter depressed you? The sexual attachments of war?

These depress me also.

Since the death of my sons, a result of wars long ago, I am even more depressed.

Let me talk to God. I will plead for a different world, who knows, he may grant it. Has a woman been allowed to ask? I would like to believe God would listen.

CHAPTER XIV
DAVID SLEEPS WITH HIS FATHERS
No longer is he tempted.
(Michal' sees the human side of eternity)

DAVID'S BEAUTY SIDE AND HIS LAST DAYS.
David is not all bad, as I may have pictured him, there is something special in him, that which God sees and uses, probably the greatest I've known in my ups and downs (What of Palti? Oh, Palti!). David's writings reveal a portion of purity, a cry for worship. If you have never heard his plea, follow me here:

"The Lord is my rock, and my fortress, and my deliverer,
my God, my rock, in whom I take refuge,
my shield and the horn of my salvation,
my stronghold and my refuge, my savior;
thou savest me from violence.
I call upon the Lord, who is worthy to be praised,
and I am saved from my enemies."

After hearing these words, how can one doubt his heart?
If only he could have kept his heart and his deeds together.
If only he could have kept the purity and singleness of purpose of his youth.
I loved that David.

There is yet some to be told. As you have followed this, you know that now David is old, his time is short, those who aspire to the throne worm their way into his presence for anointing.
Ab'salom, favorite of David, could not wait and lost his life, along with sure appointment.

My sons were eliminated at a single stroke, agreed to by David, without thought of consequences or of others involved – or, did David consider this another stroke of genius, a way to eliminate a distasteful family line? Oh, I know, they were not in the David line, but they were in the royal line of Israel's kings.

The most beautiful of his wives (you thought I could not say that), and possibly the most crafty was the *one who gained a promise that her beautiful, talented son Solomon would follow him. Or who lied to make David believe he had promised when he was young.*
One other beauty demonstrated equal guile in being added to his harem.
When the time came, even with the claimed earlier promise, the throne almost got away from him and would have except for timely intercession of his mother, Bathshe'ba.

We are ahead of ourselves, another event must be told that reflects David's character and relationship with God.
A mighty pestilence came on Israel, which David took blame for with God, seventy thousand men were numbered fallen to it. Many, many more women and even more children fell also, it was a terrible plague destroying the people of Israel. *Of course, only men were counted, because only men count.*
Two facets of David are elevated here: his surety that God controls every event of life, and his willingness to take blame to save his people.
Once more I ask for a picture of a gentler God, not one who would kill *five hundred thousand people* for one man's or two men's disobedience, one who sees human beings as worthy, not just men.
Though once again I ask mercy ... God has spoken to David, not to me.
With all my wishing for gentler things, I have done little to change the course of Israel, the course of the king's household, possibly, but not the nation. David has.

As we return to the succession to the crown of David, let us first see David's last days. They reflect the image he has built with the people of Israel.

Even in old age, David was loved by his people, the next incident shows their care and thought for him. He was ill and cold, they continually covered him with little results. Finally, a scheme was devised that was sure to do the job, considering his life-long habits.

"So they sought for a beautiful maiden throughout all the territory of Israel, and found Ab'ishag the Shunammite, and brought her to the king. The maiden was very beautiful; and she became the king's nurse and ministered to him; but the king knew her not." David finally was beyond that interest. It was long in coming.

Although David had promised the throne to another, his son Adoni'jah by his wife Haggith exalted himself and succeeded temporarily in moving up. When Bathshe'ba heard this, she went to David with a reminder of his promise to her and her son, *"My lord, you swore to your maidservant by the Lord your God, saying, 'Solomon your son shall reign after me, and he shall sit upon my throne,' and now behold Adoni'jah is king, although you, my lord, do not know it."*

Her petition was granted, apparently he had not completely forgotten his former interests, or he truly felt Solomon to be the chosen of God. *Another that no one will ever know the answer to.*

In those his last days, David tapped the deepest well within himself when he advised Solomon, the new king: *"I am about to go the way of the earth. Be strong and show yourself a man, and keep the charge of the Lord your God."*

CHAPTER XV
LOVE AND REVENGE
SHARE THE SAME TENT
Do they share the same pasture?

"Then David slept with his fathers and was buried in the city of David." He had reigned over Israel and Judah forty years.

Once again my life changed, but that is not important, except to me.

Since I know these first years of Solomon's reign, we will consider some results of David's decision to pass over older sons in favor of Bathshe'ba's oldest surviving son. You'll remember, the first died at birth.

One of Solomon's early decisions established him as ruthless when he thought it to be in his interest. This is how it happened:

His half brother Adonijah, the son of Haggith, came to Solomon's mother Bathshe'ba to intercede with her request that the king grant to him beautiful Abishag, the Shunammite, who had been David's last nurse, who had not subjected to David's lust, *she didn't need to, it was gone.*

She agreed to approach her son the king on Adonijah's behalf in the matter.

Solomon remembered Adonijah's abortive attempt to gain the throne and read into the request much more than appears on the surface (consider his interests and the beauty of Abishag).

Adonijah underestimated his brother, or he would not have asked the favor.

Solomon's reply, *"And why do you ask Ab'ishag the Shunammite for Adoni'jah? Ask for him the kingdom also; for he is my elder brother, and on his side are Abi'athar the priest and Jo'ab the son of Zeruiah." Even though he had promised to grant her request, he promptly ordered the death of his brother Adonijah.* The order was carried out without delay.

Quickly Solomon followed up with orders for the death of army commander Jo'ab who had supported Adonijah for king, earlier. He, too, was swift victim.

Others he ordered to remain within the confines of their own homes for life with sentence of death if they ventured forth.

I cannot say the appointment of Solomon was wrong, for he has reigned well.

He has held the kingdom together, judged wisely – though sometimes mercilessly, has written beautiful songs, built the temple to God.

Already he has gone far beyond kings before him with wives, concubines, and children beyond numbering.

He may have surpassed all who came before and all who will come after. So many have entered his private-quarters-become-tremendous, hardly anyone could number them. Many were foreign women, whom God had warned against.

THE OLD CRONE REFLECTS

I said earlier in these thoughts that "I am, or was, attractive." That was long ago.

No one would recognize me now; even David would not know this wrinkled crone. Again I am the old woman who accompanied the band of soldiers searching for David's camp. Then it was easy to return to being the young woman, attractive to men. Now I hope I am attractive to God. Papa was wrong about me concerning things of the spirit.

As for David, he is the one central in most of these ramblings. What would I say about him now, final comments?

I remember him as the beautiful boy-man, neither all good nor all bad.

His passions were great, both for things of the flesh and for God, he will be remembered for both, though now the beauty of his longing for God more and more lights our memories of him.

What about his selection as king? The event that thrust him

forward, felling Goliath, signaled his greatness. Nothing about David's life or reign was small, God would not have chosen a lesser one.

Would I have chosen him king? I don't know, Palti might have done better, I did not appreciate him until too late.

What of Merab, was her great declaration wasted when she denied David?

No such statement is wasted, the ripples echo in the heart of time and our people yet today. The gift of her sons to me, after I took advantage of her sacrifice of David, was an expression of love without resentment. Somehow she knew I needed them, those boys became the beauty of my life, greater than David's early love.

David robbed me of them twice, first when he removed me from their home without purpose, for he didn't want or need me. Second, when he gave them to be murdered, with that he went too far, my mind never worked the same again.

He knew what he was doing to me, he was not stupid. Yes, he was stupid if he thought he would break me with that. It would have, had he not made the mistake earlier of giving me a vocation in his household managing his harem and their offspring, giving me a purpose in life.

I managed the household in the same fashion as did mama, with no more influence on the nation than she had, but it filled my needs. Without it, I would have taken my life – or his.

In the end I did, though no one suspected, no one, that is, except God, and the one who joined in the act. With that I may have sealed my fate.

You thought David died of natural causes? Others at the time did not question because his death was expected. Why not wait, then, do you not know?

His beautiful nurse Abishag and I worked together. She had counted on his attentions to gain her advantages, when David ignored her, it was easy to get her assistance.

As he saw me standing behind Abishag, his eyes widened, but it was too late. He lost little, possibly a few days.

My boys and I watched as he walked the same divide. His eyes

mirrored them awaiting his arrival, all five of them – Merab's boys – my boys, and Palti's;
   With them stood Rizpah's two sacrificed sons;
   Nabal, rich husband of Ab'igail;
   Uriah, the Hittite warrior husband of Bathshe'ba;
   and thousands who died needlessly.
   We gained revenge and lost the peace we sought.
   For that act, for that brief satisfaction, likely I will suffer isolation from God while David basks in the glory of heaven:
   He with the blood of thousands on his hands,
   He with wives and concubines stolen from other men,
   He that asked forgiveness of God, and likely got it.

As yet I have not been able to ask forgiveness of that from which I gain so much satisfaction. That may be the difference between us, David repents his sins and asks forgiveness, even when he sometimes continues in them afterward.
   Solomon's birth was one result of such continued sin. His succession to the throne another.
   (I do not understand that, God. You rewarded evil, or did You allow Solomon's birth and events to take their own course? I am confused, God. But who understands all things, unless it is Yourself, possibly even You are puzzled about some of our thoughts and actions.)
   Rizpah fought off the carrion eaters from our sons' bodies, while David ignored that which he so indifferently caused.
   He never saw me, I went into a cave, retching with dry agony, she and I with like pain, differently expressed. When I came out, I was outwardly calm, never once did he see my hurt, until he saw me behind Abishag, but then he knew.
   Did I know a man after David's last visit to me? We have not discussed that and will not. God knows and I know, that is enough for now.
   My time is short, I am too old to care. If I have not alienated God with my ramblings, soon He may satisfy my curiosity of why certain things happen as they do. Certainly He will tell me if I can be forgiven for rejoicing in revenge. Almost do I grow repentant for

hurting David, but then I remember what he did, I never heard that he repented of that.

Please offer sacrifices for my repentance, for I know I will not see God without it.

May God, also, satisfy your curiosity and grant you peace of heart, You and I may yet see each other again. If you are still curious about my later habits, you may ask me then.

Oh, why not now? I was true to Palti in spirit – the only one who was true to me, though neither would I have gone to him, nor would I have left him, if given a choice.

As with other things, I must leave those to God, believing he understands, I have a seeking heart – which I believe God knows, I would leave it there ... but I cannot.

God forgive me my unwilling ... and my willing sins. There! I have done what I could not do. Forgive me, God, forgive papa, forgive David. Yes, I loved papa Saul very much – I, of all his children, most like him.

David? I thought I loved him. Now, comparing it to papa, it is more like infatuation. What is love? Mama is love. Yes, dull, wonderful mama; I miss her so.

One question has not been dealt with adequately: Did David love me?

I would prefer to dodge that question, but I am beyond even that, finally, I have been able to face the truth; *in all likelihood he did not.* Why do I say that?

The man of a thousand songs never sang to me.

We never talked of my dreams, my needs, as though I had none; it was always David, David who would be king, finally David king of all Israel. In the end, my love for my boys didn't matter to him; their lives were a means to satisfy a gap in himself, his wants, his career.

In later years, my place with David was a mirror of mama with papa, except that mama never quite gave up her dreams that he would return to her love. Almost was I like mama, in the end I knew David had no interest in me.

In ways, papa was the better man, his excesses with women were always restrained in comparison to David's.

David's reached the place that everyone knew, abetted, granted him his excesses, wove them into acceptance, the hero worship in which anything he did became the pattern of his people.

Everyone knew; not everyone granted, though almost everyone. If David's songs truly brought God's acceptance of his repeated sinning, then all my searching is in vain.

One thing I hold in reservation: Since my boys, being a mother rises to a greater thrill than leading armies.

The shadow on that is: *if God smiles on men's use of women.* David did not begin that, but he painted it in new colors with his songs, mixing God's blessing into his excesses – not exactly mixing, but, in the minds of men, it was. Solomon watched, learned, took up where David ended and went to new extremes.

I try to understand ... for I am a woman, and I loved David, once.

David has woven a new pattern for tomorrow, possibly for all men to marvel at, to follow, Whatever David does, can be excused, must be right. You see, I want to believe; I do believe – I believe that God sees him as any other man. It may be too much to hope that He also sees him as He sees any woman.

Near the end, David was almost brought down by what he thought was a simple mistake, but was from one of the great flaws of his character: to him, male sexual laxity was not a serious thing. To David, Amnon's incest of his sisterr Tamar was forgivable, Ab'salom's murder of Amnon was not, *because Amnon was his son.* His decision based on faulty standards cost him his favorite son, nearly cost him his kingdom.

Did David sing to any other? How would I know that? It isn't the kind of thing he'd tell me; his others saw no reason to do so. Now it has no importance except to point out what is true, what I would have known if my heart had not been so involved.

Why, then, did he call me back? Likely it was a matter of property; even though neither his needs nor interests any longer required me, I had not been released, merely surrendered.

Even in that small way, my position with Palti was a reminder of a defeat not avenged. His vengeance could not be heaped on Saul, for he was gone; instead it was fulfilled in his own way by utterly destroying what had been built from nothing; the giving of my sons to be murdered may well have been the final satisfaction of that revenge.

Who was David? Was he evil? *Is this what my life comes to, am I boiling in bitter gall after doing what I could not do?* Was my own revenge wasted?

David was a man whose personality blazed in the night as a great campfire radiating, undulating to the uttermost darkness of the camp. In the day, he was as a wind-song woven into a rainbow, captivating with his love; then he was a raging storm, winding tentacles laced with thorns of the desert bush, flinging them about those, friend or foe, who hindered or increased his dreams and kingdoms, a whispering trace of his greatness remained to the end.

This shepherd of the mountain pastures became the warrior king who carried a lyre and a sword, king of the great Israeli people, killer of Philistines, Hittites, and other hosts, song maker, lover.

Above all, David was a man who worshipped God. He left an unmatched legacy in that for his people, for we were his people.

The questions about his perplexing shortcomings must remain. I've forgiven him all but killing my sons, for holding that, I've asked God's forgiveness. That hurt may never be removed from my heart except by death.

You have accompanied me on this search for peace. It has come at last – though without answers to questions that pummeled as a stone barrage, as David's sling flung at Goliath, except never ceasing. In the end, I accept that God uses those available, thus far none perfect, no more am I, least of all I, a woman.

Though it still disturbs me that I dwell on things that should be left to God; surely His priests and kings will tell us what He wants us to know. That is part of my problem, I've been too close to two of them, kings, observed their sails cant in shattering winds. Our people would make Gods of their leaders, but I've seen no substitute Gods.

Why must He speak to us through men's weakness?

Yes, God, if I'm a woman in your house, it will not displease me.

If my plea for forgiveness is too little too late and we end in different kingdoms, you would not know these last intimacies if I did not tell you now.

Please, tell God of my searching heart if He asks. He may have grown weary and moved on to other things before hearing me out ... I cease these ramblings, for I am weary.

I struggle to pass one more thought:

As I go, I hold my only victory, after being called back to David, I locked my mind on Palti as I submitted to David, the few times he called me.

I hope we meet again, Palti, my love.

*

Printed in the United States
714600001B